# A Very Special Dress
## *& other stories*

by Aimee Herman
& Martin Herman

Published and Distributed by:
**194 Rodney Press**

**521 Simsbury Road, Bloomfield, CT 0600**

Copyright ©2017 Aimee Herman and Martin Herman

ISBN: 978-1-945211-06-5 PRINT

First Printing - September, 2017
Printed in the United States of America

Creative Editorial Consultant: Allan Pepper
Cover design/Graphics: Deborah E. Gordon
Copy Editor/Layout: Ed de la Garza

ALL RIGHTS RESERVED. No part of this book publication may be reproduced, stored in a retrieval system, or transmitted in any form or by any means – electronic, mechanical, photo-copy, recording, or any other – except brief quotation in reviews, without the prior permission of the author or publisher.

This is a work of fact inspired fiction. Names, characters, businesses, places, events and incidents are included with the full and unconditional permission of those involved; some details may have been enhanced by the author's imagination or used in a fictitious manner. Any resemblance to persons other than the main characters, living or dead, or other events is purely coincidental.

Subjects: Relationships--Marriage, Gender Identity, Immigrants, Sexual Orientation, Death/Dying, Friendships, Pets | Creative Non-Fiction, Autobiographical Fiction, and Magical Realism

ALSO BY AIMEE HERMAN
Poetry:
*carpus, chapbook (essay press)*
*meant to wake up feeling (great weather for MEDIA)*
*rooted, chapbook (dancing girl press)*
*to go without blinking (BlazeVOX books)*


ALSO BY MARTIN HERMAN
*The Jefferson Files*
*The Jefferson Files - the expanded edition*
*The Hidden Treasure Files*
*The Sweet Revenge Files*

# Table of Contents

- 1   Happily Ever After??? *(Author's Forward)*
- 4   'L' is For the Way You Look at Me *(Author's Forward)*
- 11   A Very Special Dress
- 21   Finding Love at a Perfume Counter
- 29   Once Upon a Time There Was a Wart
- 49   Howie and Sandy
- 64   The Chair
- 78   What Happens When You Wait
- 81   The Legalization of Marriage
- 83   Home
- 85   No Need for Subtitles
- 98   Frangelico
- 107   Hibernation
- 114   Shelly and Greg: An Almost Love Story
- 132   First Date
- 142   The lovely Lora ...
- 146   Schadenfreude
- 160   Dragonflies
- 167   Norma Jean
- 180   Rats v. Pigeons
- 190   My Father
- 199   A Correspondence Between Two Writers

Aimee Herman and Martin Herman

# **Happily Ever After???**

One day, I passed an elderly couple holding hands while sitting on a park bench. I introduced myself as someone who was in the process of writing a book about relationships ... loves found ... loves lost ... loves that might have been. I asked them to describe love to me in as few words as possible.

The man smiled, "If you are as old as you look and you still need a complete stranger like me to describe love to you, well, you must have lived a very empty life."

The woman was a bit more indulgent. "I cannot give you a general answer; I can only answer for myself. Knowing what love is can be less a simple definition and more a result of our experiences. When I met Archie, I was sunning myself on a beach and all I saw were well-defined abs, a full head of wavy blond hair and the bluest blue eyes I had ever seen. I knew right then and there that I was meant to be with him forevermore."

I turned to the man, pointed to the woman and said, "Tell me Archie, did you have a similar reaction when you first met her?"

He laughed and said, "I'm not Archie; Archie was her first husband."

The woman quickly added, "I was 16 at the time, it was only natural for my eyes and hormones to define love for me. Eventually, my brain took over and that was when I knew that the guy sharing this bench with me today was the one and only for me. He is my definition of love. We all have to love at least one bad partner during our early years in order to be able to recognize the right one when he or she finally shows up."

This collection of short stories and poems may not be the definitive description of what love is any better than the one I got from the woman on the bench, but if it makes you think about how you would answer the question, then this book is all I hoped it could be.

*Martin Herman,*
*Bloomfield, CT*

# 'L' is for the Way You Look at Me

Natalie Cole resurrected her father in order to sing about it. It's been captured on billboards and public art, carved into wet cement and permanently inked on bathroom walls. When I was a kid, I couldn't wait to fall in love. I didn't feel it for the first time until I was 18. Glimpses of it before then and, of course, it grew heavier and thicker as I moved into my 20s and 30s.

Last year, when I engaged in something I never thought I would (or legally could) — MARRIAGE — I reflected on all the versions of love I've experienced in my life, and how *this* one was different. Love is not just related to sex and intimacy. Love can also be experienced in friendships and there are glimpses of it felt through encounters with strangers. When we learn more about ourselves through our interactions with others, there is potential for love.

I thought about the myriad of humans I've encountered in my life that helped me remain here. The ones who asked me all the right questions to guide me into my own personal dig. This could be the perfect moment where I write: *The ones who helped me learn how to love myself.* But even though I don't know you, dear reader, I want to start out this book being 100 percent honest. I'm not quite there yet. Every day, I work toward trying to understand myself better. But even though I've known myself for almost 40 years (!!!), there are times I still feel like a stranger to myself. Through these stories, fictional and real encounters, I am collecting a vocabulary toward liking myself. Love (for me) will come later.

I am a huge fan of origin stories. At my sister's 40th birthday party, I recall asking several of her friends (mostly married couples), how they met. I loved watching them watch each other fill in memories and the moments that completely changed their lives. So many people meet online now; it's a great opportunity to shop a catalogue of smiles and shared interests.

But the poet in me prefers more chance encounters. I've been lucky. I met my first love at a movie theater (where I worked as her manager). The next one I met while studying at a summer writing program in Northampton, Massachusetts. During an assignment of writing down bits of overheard conversation, I grew mesmerized by his enthusiastic cadence. It was a summer of discovering each other's language, which led into many more months of me trying to understand what it meant that as a lesbian, I was falling in love with a man. Years later, I am able to articulate that gender and sexuality is more than just a box we check off. It is far more complicated.

After that, there was another love who encouraged me to be wild (though sometimes that led to some not-so-safe decisions). And then the big one. If we are lucky, we get many big loves in our life. I've been lucky to have two.

The first one I met while studying writing and poetics in Colorado. She was tall, a Canadian, and the deepest thinker I had ever met. She asked me questions that twirled around me like a second coat of skin. Through her, I learned how to give away my secrets. Through her, I learned how to find even more of my wild.

I used to worry that I gave my heart away too easily. It is a muscle, so it can build up once it is torn down, but it still hurts when it's broken. I desperately tried to build a cage big enough to lock it away, out of sight, out of harm's way.

Then I met the one I later married. And I knew he was the one before I could finish exhaling my first breath beside him.

I came out as a lesbian when I was 19 years old. That word has since shifted around to fit my ever-growing gender and sexual identity, but I knew then that I would never get married. Back then, it wasn't legal. In 2003, Massachusetts became the first U.S. state to sanction it. On June 26, 2015, the U.S. Supreme Court finally legalized gay marriage in all 50 states. I remember receiving messages from friends so excited to hear this news. I cried, feeling the history of all the LGBTQ folks and allies who fought for this right that should have been in place all along.

When my partner proposed, I did not say yes immediately. Love is complicated and scary and I've said yes and no too many times in my life without fully digesting the meaning wrapped around the question. What does marriage even mean? I didn't have many strong examples around me. So many divorces and affairs and unhappiness and ... and ... and. What we shared was so magical; did I want to tarnish it by getting the government involved? I know, I know ... more than 1,000 benefits to being married. But that's not a good enough reason to get married. So what is ...

*Love?*

After 20 minutes (or so), I said YES. One year later, we were married and we've been redefining this word ever since.

The stories and poems in this book span generations and sexual orientations and even involve the love of a dog. There is no one way to love and who is really qualified to denounce anyone's version of it? This world can be so challenging and painful to exist inside, so shouldn't we encourage all versions of love? Read on ...

*Aimee Herman,*
*Brooklyn, New York*

Aimee Herman and Martin Herman

# A Very Special Dress

Evelyn Zaleson was the youngest of eight children. Like most parents in America during the 1930s, for Evelyn's father, the newly naturalized citizen Jacob Zaleson, the overriding objective was to provide a dry roof over his family's heads, plenty of food for the table, and the very best for his children. Unfortunately, Jacob was limited in what he could provide by his meager earnings from a slaughterhouse as an assembly line butcher.

His American born wife, Marsha, many years his junior, was a stay-at-home mom. Together, they prioritized the needs of their four sons, because sons could always be expected to support and care for their parents in their old age. By comparison, they believed that their only responsibility to their four daughters was to actively search out rich husbands for them.

One by one, Evelyn watched her older siblings be introduced and married off to their life partners and begin raising families of their own. "When will it be my turn?" she kept asking.

Then she met Benjamin.

Evelyn began spending her afternoons at the small soda fountain-luncheonette-newspaper stand on the street where she lived. Benjamin worked there with his father and mother. Evelyn had a crush on Benjamin the minute she saw him, and he really liked the attention he was getting from this spirited young girl.

The store opened, like clockwork, every morning at 5 o'clock, seven days a week, rain or shine and everything in between. Benjamin's father usually opened the store by 7 a.m. and closed it around 11 p.m.; his wife and son Benjamin joined him at 8 a.m. After the last morning rush, Benjamin took over so that his parents could go home and rest.

That was until *that girl,* which was how Benjamin's mother referred to Evelyn, began stalking her beloved son, Benny. As soon as Benjamin's mother became aware of Evelyn's daily visits, she made sure she was sitting by the window, in front of the cash register whenever he was working. Her glares and harsh mumblings either didn't register with Evelyn or just fed Evelyn's hopes that one day the dislike would turn to love in her favor. However, with or without the maternal acceptance, as she told her sisters, *"nothing ... no one ... was going to keep me from my man!"*

One evening, as Benjamin's father was locking up, two young toughs grabbed the brown paper bag with the day's cash and began beating the old man. The father did what he could to resist, but in the struggle, was savagely beaten and died in the ambulance on the way to the hospital. From that point on, Benjamin and his mother ran the store. The mother left around 4 p.m. each day to go home and make supper, which she brought to Benjamin by 6 p.m. sharp. Evelyn became a fixture on the third stool of the long fountain during those two glorious hours.

Eventually, a romance bloomed and Benjamin proposed. He twisted a piece of wire into the shape of a ring and gently placed it around her finger. Evelyn accepted before the words had even left his lips. He asked her to keep it a secret for a while but she couldn't wait to tell her sisters; within minutes word spread throughout the neighborhood.

Evelyn began working on her parents to give their permission and Benjamin did the same with his mother. The Zalesons warmly welcomed their soon to be son-in-law into their family. Benjamin's mother was upset when she first heard the news, but eventually she too accepted the inevitable. With a heavy sigh, she gave her approval and with the look of one who had just consumed the juice of a dozen lemons, air-kissed her soon to be daughter-in-law somewhere in the general area of her cheek.

A wedding date could now be set.

There was very, very, very little money available from either side and so it was understood that there would be a very small wedding, followed by a luncheon. Only the immediate family members would be invited. One of Evelyn's brothers knew someone who knew someone who worked in Gluckstern's Kosher Restaurant on the lower east side of New York City. Somehow, the owner of Gluckstern's was persuaded to drastically cut the cost of the luncheon and Evelyn's four brothers chipped in to pay for it.

Evelyn's dream was to have a new wedding dress and a separate dress for the reception luncheon, but that was not to be. A relative offered to provide a wedding dress that was either taken in or let out many different times in the past. The most important two facts about *this* dress was that every bride who wore it enjoyed long and possibly happy marriages, and each of those marriages produced multiple babies. Other than hopeless Annie, the black sheep of the family, none had been widowed at an early age. A neighbor reshaped the dress to fit this bride-to-be. The shoes came from one of Evelyn's older sisters.

Another sister advised Evelyn that it was just bad luck to start a marriage without *something* new and so together they decided that there must be — at the very least — a new dress for the luncheon. Evelyn worked several jobs and ultimately saved enough for — as she called it — a fancy, shmancy, knock-them-dead dress for the post-ceremony luncheon.

The search for a dress began at Macy's, then Gimble Brothers, then John

Wanamaker's but there was absolutely no doubt that the ultimate purchase would be made at Lord & Taylor. Although there were a few nice dresses at the other stores, Evelyn just knew that she would find the dress of her dreams at Lord & Taylor ... and she did.

She brought one of her sisters to the store to see the dress and her sister agreed, "This dress is worth living on bread and water for a month — if you have to."

They talked to the sales clerk; Evelyn was positioned on a small platform and stood erect as a friendly seamstress pinned and chalk-marked the dress to accent Evelyn's curves. A small deposit was left and Evelyn agreed to return later that week with the money.

Three days later, in the subway on their way back to the store, someone stole Evelyn's purse. She broke down in tears, reflecting on all she had done just to make this purchase possible.

Realizing that she would never be able to come up with more money, she went back to the store to tell the sales clerk that she would not be able to finalize the purchase.

Typical of better department stores of that day, the sales clerk expressed more concern for Evelyn's broken spirit than for losing this sale. Within minutes, Evelyn was surrounded by the store manager and several other clerks. The manager offered to accept the small down payment for the dress, but Evelyn refused. That would be charity, and charity was no way to begin a new life with her wonderful Benjamin. Ultimately, it was agreed that she would be allowed to work off the full price of the dress as a part timer ... which she did.

The manager threw in a pair of shoes and the clerks chipped in to pay for a pair of nylons — which in pre-war America was more valuable than gold — especially to a young woman about to be married.

Although she never wore the dress out of her apartment ever again, whenever she felt down or sad, she would sit in front of her closet and look at it. The dress hung in her clothes closet on a cloth trimmed padded hanger, in a heavy see-through plastic garment bag along with her wedding flower bouquet, until the day she died.

---

***Author's note:*** *My mother told me this story a few days before my own wedding. It helped me to understand why Lord & Taylor always held such a special place in her heart.*

*For several weeks before the wedding day, my mother continually suggested that I purchase a new dress from Lord & Taylor for my wife-to-be to take on our honeymoon. At first, I told her that my wife-to-be prefers to pick out her own clothes. Then I told her that she had her own tastes in clothing. Finally, I just ignored the suggestion. As the hour grew closer, her comments became louder. When it was clear that she needed to help me understand her motives, she sat me down and began to tell me the story, as she remembered it, of her very special dress.*

*M.H.*

Aimee Herman and Martin Herman

# Finding Love at a Perfume Counter

## As he remembers it:

"I don't think I was ever in a Lord & Taylor Department Store before that morning. Hey, they call themselves *the dress address* — what did I know about dresses?

"I just wanted to run in and buy my mother a Mother's Day gift and then, just as quickly, get back to work. I was actually heading toward the almost endless showcase of watches when I was stopped in my tracks by some person, a blur of movement, who pushed a small white card at me and said, 'It's our newest fragrance — she'll love you for buying it for her.'"

## *As she remembers it:*

*"I was a demonstrator for Chanel. My job was to mindlessly pass out*

*perfume scented cards. I noticed him instantly; he seemed to be preoccupied and dumbstruck at the very same time. It was clear to me that he was very uncomfortable being in a store with so many women and women's things.*

*"I handed him one of the scented cards and said something like, 'this is our newest fragrance, it happens to be on sale today.' Then I probably said the same thing I was trained to say to all male customers in order to increase the chances to get them to buy a bottle; I used to practice the line in front of the mirror at home until it sounded like I never said it before: 'She will fall in love with you all over again if you present it to her.'*

*"When I said it to him, he blushed, grabbed the card, and scurried away like a little school boy."*

## As he remembers it:

"I shoved the card into my shirt pocket and went over to look at the watches. Nothing really hit me as one my Mom would likely wear, and since I was already late for an appointment, I rushed out of the store.

"For the rest of the day, the scent from the card wafted up at me from my shirt pocket. It kept reminding me of the sales clerk.

"Early the next day, I went back to the store, this time, looking for the sales clerk, but she wasn't there.

"I thought I would try one more time, and this time, when I entered the store, there she was, stunning, more than *just* pretty, there was a natural charm and glow that made me feel warm all over just looking at her.

"I said, 'Hi! Remember me?' Without a moment's hesitation she said, 'Of course I do.'"

## *As she remembers it:*

*"The next time I saw him was maybe a few weeks later. I noticed someone staring at me from the next aisle. Eventually, he walked closer to me and showed me a scented card, similar to the hundreds of cards I passed out during an eight-hour shift that time of year.*

*"He said something like, 'Remember me?'*

*"Frankly, I didn't remember him. After all, this was Lord & Taylor; I spoke to a lot of people every day and he was just one of many. But, not wanting to hurt his feelings, I told him that I did remember him.*

*"He asked me if I still had the same perfume on sale.*

*"I told him that the sale ended a day or two before but thought that the manager might be willing to honor the sale price. I excused myself and went over to the department manager. She gave me permission to honor the sale price. I went back to the man and told him.*

*"The man handed me his American Express card. I remember it was a gold American Express card — I had never seen one of those before; I thought they only issued those cards in green. It really made an impression on me.*

*"He asked me to gift wrap it and on the gift card put my own name.*

*"I told him that would be against store policy — frankly, I didn't know if it was or wasn't against policy but I didn't like where this conversation was going.*

*"He said he understood and asked me to gift wrap it. I did as he asked and processed his card for payment.*

*"He then left, or so I thought.*

*"Minutes later, one of the other clerks came over to me, handed me the giftwrapped package and said that someone asked her to personally deliver it to me. His business card was attached with a brief note on the back.*

*"I saved his note — I cannot explain why, but I did. In fact, I still have it to this day."*


## As he remembers it:

"I asked her out the next day and she said yes and we have been together ever since."

## *As she remembers it:*

*"He came back the next day and began stuttering; he finally asked if I would like to break away for a cup of coffee. I told him that I was on the clock and couldn't get away. Meanwhile, I was thinking, is this some kind of stalker?*

*"Fortunately, a shopper walked over to ask a question. He looked befuddled and smiled awkwardly. He mumbled something like see you around, and quickly left the store.*

*"An hour or so later, close to the end of my shift he returned. He asked again if I would join him for a cup of coffee. I told him I had to get home after the shift, but would be willing to spend a few minutes at the coffee shop in the mall after I clocked out.*

*"My basic instincts told me that nothing good could come from this but he did buy me a very expensive bottle of*

*perfume, so I said yes. And that few-minutes coffee conversation has lasted until this day.*

*"Last Sunday was our 10th wedding anniversary. We went back to the Lord & Taylor store during lunchtime, went directly up to the café, and repeated our wedding vows all over again.*

*"Go figure."*

M.H.

Aimee Herman and Martin Herman

# Once Upon a Time There Was a Wart

## Chapter 1

Jolene knew everything there was to know about herself. She sneezed in increments of three. Her metabolism was moody, and often held onto things long enough to create swell and button-pop. Her hair was thicker than most, but fell out in impressive clumps after each shower, persistently clogging up the drain. She preferred collars to V-necks; loathed the taste of coffee-flavored anything, and preferred an unmade bed. She could spend an entire day speaking to no one. Because of this, her breath was charred and stale, barely getting out much. She lived in a small town where nothing new happened.

She had memorized the cloud formations lingering over buildings. The crime rate was non-existent because no one really had much to steal. But she liked it here, where doors remained unlocked and doorbells often stayed silent. There were absolutely no surprises.

## Chapter 2

Tuesday through Friday, Jolene walks to the library, leaving her home at 8:45 am to arrive by 9. As she walks, nothing catches her eye because nothing has changed. The grass is no greener today than yesterday. The flowers are not miraculous in scent or color. Birds fly here just like anywhere else, and though there are squirrels, they tend to keep to themselves too. At work, she shelves neglected books, absorbing bits of information as she skims from each one. Usually, she flips to a page, reads a paragraph and then, based upon last name, houses it beside its alphabetical letter mates.

Her co-workers are uneventful. Margery is plump, married, and lingers beside the romance books. Jolene has nothing against love or that sort of thing, but she's just never had that feeling before.

"It lives in your stomach," Margery had said. "Fluttery butterflies. And then you just know ... you're in love." Perhaps this is why Margery's belly is so extensive; it is simply full of romance.

There is also Pamela, Yusuf, Dee, and Frank. Jolene has no opinions on any of them.

## Chapter 3

Jolene wakes alone, just like every other day. Her hair is almost unruffled; she barely moves much once her eyes are closed. She gets out of her bed, leaving her sheets and heavy comforter alone. Her breakfast is whatever is easiest to put inside her: a small cup of yogurt, muffin (on sale at grocery store due to expiration date), or a piece of fruit.

When she walks the few steps to her bathroom, she almost doesn't see it. She has been staring at her face for 52 years and nothing really surprises her anymore.

"Hello," it whispers.

Jolene gasps, looking behind her. She hasn't had a guest in her home for more than two years. Not since the funeral, when all her family — much of which hadn't seen each other in a decade — stomped into her home in search of the traditional post-funeral spread. All she had to offer were some withered grapes and individual slices of processed cheese.

"H-hello?" she dribbles out of her still-sleepy lips.

"Good morning," it says.

"Now, who is speaking? I want to know," she demands.

Jolene does not believe in ghosts, God, or dinosaurs.

"It's me," she hears.

Jolene turns on the bathroom light and looks into the mirror. She does not have to squint her eyes or move any closer to her reflection in order to see it. It was certainly not there yesterday, and she couldn't understand how it had just grown overnight, but on the left side of her cheek, an inch below her eye, was a giant wart.

Generally, Jolene's beauty regime consisted of brushing her teeth, finger-combing her hair and putting on clothes. She wore no make-up, nor spent any time on nonsense like face creams or pore-reducers.

"Did you sleep OK?" it asks.

"*Who* is speaking?"

"Me."

Jolene jumps, feeling her ribs rattle just a bit. If she hadn't been staring in the mirror at that moment, she would not have believed it.

The voice was coming from the wart.

"I ... I do not believe in this."

"You do not believe in what?" the wart asks.

"*This. You.* A wart talking to me!"

"Well, that's OK. I understand; I am uninvited. I happened while you were sleeping. You sleep so ... gracefully." The wart blushes. "I mean, you don't twist or turn. Your face just turns off. Your skin becomes like water, almost."

"I can't believe this. I just—"

"It's Saturday, isn't it?" the wart asks.

"What? Yes, but—"

"I'd ask if you'd like to spend some time with me, but that's kind of inevitable," the wart chuckles. "But ... would you?"

Usually, Jolene's weekends were just as uneventful as the rest of her days. She woke, ate breakfast, watched her programs until her eyes hurt, and then napped. Sometimes she'd read. Sometimes, she'd take a short walk. Jolene was not fond of deviations from this regime.

"Spend the day with you? Doing what?"

"Anything," the wart says. "I just want to get to know you better."

## Chapter 4

The wart asks her questions about herself that no one ever bothered to wonder. It wanted to know what stopped her from being drowned by tears after her father died.

"I started taking books out that I knew he'd like. Stories he'd want to read. It made me feel closer to him."

It asked why she parted her hair down the middle (she didn't; it just fell that way). It asked her what she thought about the sky.

"What do you mean? It's a sky. I don't have any thoughts about it."

"But the color and the way that you can't really call it blue. Because it's like calling *water* blue, but it isn't. Water is a reflection. Just like me," the wart says.

"*You're* a reflection?"

"I'm part of you, aren't I?"

Jolene thinks about this for a minute. She's really not used to so much talking. She gathers up her spit and swallows, noting the altered flavor. Her breath and saliva taste more alive than it ever has.

"I think it's big," she says. "The sky, I mean. I guess I have always just dismissed it as blue; and nothing special because it's there every day."

"But it changes," the wart interrupts.

"I guess."

"Like you."

"Sure," she says.

## Chapter 5

Jolene and the wart have a picnic in the small park on the edge of her town's border. She had been there a few times with her father, but hasn't been back in years.

"I like watching you eat," the wart says.

Jolene blushes.

"Tell me ... tell me what it tastes like."

"Food," she says dismissively.

The wart smiles or moves in such a way that Jolene acknowledges it as such.

"Please," the wart begs.

"Well, watermelon is my favorite summer food. It just kind of melts in your mouth and it's so delicious, so bright."

"Tell me what it tastes like."

"Sugar water, cotton candy, it's quite messy, actually." She looks down and notices that her shirt has gotten dirty from drips of the fruit.

"You seem to be enjoying it."

"I guess. I wouldn't say I really enjoy much these days."

The wart doesn't say anything for a long time. And then, "I'd like to tell you that you're beautiful."

Jolene doesn't know what to say. No one has ever told her this. Or if they have, it has been long enough that she has forgotten.

"This is all quite ridiculous," Jolene exhales.

Just then, a shadow falls over their picnic blanket. Jolene looks up.

"Why hello, Jolene," Margery is standing beside a man Jolene assumes is her husband, since they are holding hands. "Philippe, this is Jolene. We work together at the library."

"Hello," Philippe says.

"A picnic by yourself? How quaint," Margery says.

Jolene feels her entire body weighed down in shame.

"Uh ..." is all Jolene can utter.

"I guess I assumed you lived at the library," Margery chuckles. "I never see you anywhere but there."

"Y-yeah."

"Oh, honey, you've got something on your ..."

Jolene cringes.

"None of my business, Jolene, but I had a terrible growth just like that one and it turned out it was skin cancer. You should really have that looked out. It's a curable cancer, but if it's ignored—"

"Thanks, Margery," Jolene says dismissively. "Noted."

Margery and Philippe walk away and Jolene starts to pack up the small array of food she had brought.

"Wait, what are you doing?" the wart asks.

"What if she's right? What if you *are* cancer? This is all just too much. I can't believe I am sitting here having a picnic with you. With my ... wart! Stop talking to me. I much prefer being inside. Being alone. Being unbothered. How it was."

"I'm ... I'm sorry to have caused you any pain. I just thought—"

"What have I become? I'm going to make a doctor's appointment right away and get you removed."

Suddenly she felt something wet on her face. She looked up, thinking it had started to rain. She touched her cheek; the wart was crying.

"Oh, gosh. I'm ... I'm sorry," Jolene shakes her head rapidly. "And now I'm apologizing to my wart! I've gone crazy!"

"Will you take me to your favorite place?"

"What? I don't ... I don't have—"

"The bridge. By the waterfall."

"How do you even know about that? I haven't been there since my father—"

"I hear it's quite a sight," the wart says.

## Chapter 6

The sound of the water coming down against the rocks sounds like a standing ovation.

Jolene stands on the bridge, looking over the water. She inhales the moisture, the scent of earth folding itself in.

"Why don't you come here anymore?" the wart asks.

"Because all I remember is my father when I'm here and it makes me miss him more. I like my life now. Simple. Boring."

"Really? Something in me tells me that's not true."

Jolene brought her finger up to her face, grazing the wart. It was raised, almost round, and hard. Her finger backed away.

"It's OK. You can touch me," the wart says.

"I guess I stopped living after he died. I mean, I still wake, eat, go to work, that sort of thing. I just ... I stopped looking around."

"So ... start looking again. Everything has always remained. You just tuned it all out. Open your eyes."

Jolene lifts her head up, stretching her neck to take in the sky, which was no longer just blue to her, but like an inverted ocean, constantly moving. She was beginning to see what she was missing out on.

"Remember what I said earlier?" the wart says.

"Which part?"

"That you are beautiful. Silly, right? That we need to hear this from another in order to be reminded that we are."

Jolene smiles, slowly.

"So, now what? Should I get used to this?" Jolene asks.

"Which part?"

"Well, *you*. A wart. On my face. Talking to me."

"Maybe. Maybe I'll fade in a week or a month. But I don't matter. Will you remember all of *this*?"

Jolene looks around. She opens her mouth and howls. Not quite a scream, but more of a song, captured in one, jagged note. She had forgotten her voice.

"Yeah. I think I will.

## Chapter 7

Jolene decided to quit her job at the library. She would miss the smell of books in the morning, the quiet slurp of pages being turned, and Margery's heavy steps. But something in her changed and she knew it was best to turn toward a different direction for once. She had enough money saved up to go somewhere she had never been. She would never have even thought about a vacation or adventure; it had been so long since she had given herself permission to enjoy anything.

"If you could go anywhere, which place would you choose?" the wart asked.

"Mount Rushmore," she said, slightly surprised by her prompt answer.

"Well, then. Start packing."

## Chapter 8

She couldn't remember when she first learned about Mount Rushmore, but she could recall thinking how magical it was that faces had been carved into a mountain. She wanted to see the scope of its size. Of course, she had seen pictures, but seeing it with sky behind it and all the greenery around could not be truly captured by a photograph.

"I was expecting somewhere more exotic," the wart had announced.

"Yeah, maybe I was too. But I've lived in this town my whole life and it feels terrible that I've barely seen *this* country."

The wart smiled. "Listen, I'm not ... I'm not going to be here forever. We are like water, rushing in, and leaving bits behind. I—"

Jolene touched the wart, softly with her ring finger. "I know. And I cannot believe I am saying this, but I'm grateful you arrived when you did."

"It is so easy to forget how to live even when we are busy living," the wart said.

## Chapter 9

Jolene did not own any luggage, but didn't need much anyway. She packed her backpack full of what she thought were essentials, and then hopped on the bus toward the airport. She knew her destination, but was open to the possibility of getting lost. She was finally ready to be surprised again.

A.H.

Aimee Herman and Martin Herman

# Howie and Sandy

"Eighteen, 19," the petite woman sat staring at herself in the scratched mirror of her vanity as she combed her hair in long, careful strokes. "Twenty, 21; I'm still a beauty; 22, 23, 24; they have nothing on me ..."

"Who has nothing on you?" Sandy asked, as she stood by the door. She walked over to the edge of the bed and sat stiffly on the edge.

"Oh, you startled me," her mother said, sternly. "Are we to have no privacy here?"

"Who, Momma, who has nothing on you?"

"What are you babbling about?" the woman asked. "I don't like when you sneak up on me like that."

"You said someone had nothing on you. What are you talking about? And why are you talking to yourself in the mirror?"

"The Gabors," she said dismissively. "Especially Zsa Zsa, that Hungarian slut. I was talking about the Gabors. They think they are so glamorous, but they have nothing on me."

Sandy smiled. *She's in her own little world again,* Sandy thought. She took a deep breath, slowly exhaled and then said, "We're getting married, Mama."

"Twenty-five, 26. What did you say? Speak up."

"We are getting married," Sandy repeated.

"*We?* Who is we?"

Another deep breath and slow exhale, "We, is me and Howie."

"You and whom? I asked you to speak up."

"Me and Howie."

"Oh," the old woman chuckled. "I thought you said Howie."

"I did say Howie."

"Too bad." Her mother carefully inspected her hairbrush. She plucked several loose hairs from the bristles, rolled the accumulated hairs into a ball and carefully placed the hairball into the small trash basket on the floor next to her seat. "Have you set a date?"

"Yes, we will be getting married in three months."

"Three months from when?"

"Three months from now."

"From now? What's the hurry?" She dropped her hairbrush and turned to face her daughter. "Sandra Madeline Palmer, are you pregnant?"

"No," Sandy laughed, "I'm not pregnant."

"I wouldn't put it past him. I told you, he is a no good nick, he'll never amount to anything."

"Whatever you might think of him, Howie will soon be my husband and *your* son-in- law."

"Ptoo," the old woman said, dismissively. "I don't know what you see in him. So, you say you aren't pregnant, so then, what is the rush? I need time to prepare. I don't know what upsets me more, that you are hitching your wagon to that no good nick or that you are rushing into a wedding so quickly that I don't have the necessary time to do it right."

She picked up the brush and then staring at her daughter through the vanity mirror she added, "Of course I know what upsets me more. It is that you feel the need to marry him at all. Three months? No, it can't be in three months. I need time; I have to buy a dress, I need to make an appointment at the beauty parlor. Tony is always booked up so far in advance — and the hall — you will never get a good place to hold the reception in just three months; no, it can't be in three months. I need to do too much and three months will just not do."

She picked up the brush again. "Where was I, oh yes, 27, 28, 20- ... I will have to buy invitation cards, that all takes time. Until the cards are printed — I can't even invite that many friends ... relatives ... and the neighbors ... they need proper notice ... you can't just think they are waiting at the mailbox for your invitation. These people have lives. How am I going to do all of that in three months?"

"We want a very small wedding, Mama."

"My only chance to be the mother-of-the-bride and she wants to exclude some of our friends and relatives and neighbors. So thoughtless," Sandy's mother said to her image in the mirror. "So who do you want me to exclude?"

"Everyone. We only want the immediate family."

"Our friends and family and neighbors *are* our immediate family."

"This is how we want it."

"OK, OK, so I won't invite the out-of-town relatives. This will make them very angry — don't expect a gift from them."

"Please don't make this so difficult for me, Mama."

"Difficult for whom; stop thinking only about yourself; I'm not making it difficult for you," her mother said, turning again to look at her daughter. "OK, so tell me, how many people are you planning to invite?"

"Nine."

The mother laughed, "From the sublime to the ridiculous ... nine. We know hundreds, maybe thousands of people and you want to invite just nine. What are you planning to do, walk with your head down for the rest of your life because you so inconsiderately ignored them from your wedding?"

"Nine, Mama, the nine most important people in my life, n-i-n-e, nine. We only want the nine people who mean the most to us; you and dad, Howie's parents, his brother and his fiancé, Marilyn, maybe my best friend in the entire world, and of course, Howie and me. That's nine.

Howie isn't even going to invite *his* best friend in the entire world."

"So you *are* pregnant."

Sandy's face turned bright red. "I'm not pregnant, Mama. It's just that times are a little tough right now." She paused, hesitating to tell her mother the rest. "Howie just ... lost his job."

"So how are you two going to live?"

"We'll live, I'm sure we will live. With him, I never worry. I feel calm. Taken care of."

"Why not wait a while, at least until he finds a new job. I just don't understand why you must get married now?"

"Probably for the same reason you and dad got married. We love each other."

"Love, shmuv; first of all, don't compare yourself to me. *I* was a real beauty. I could have had my pick."

Her mother turned back toward the mirror, a deep sigh followed by an even deeper sigh. "It's your life, do what you want. It won't last you know, money problems are too often the root of broken marriages."

She picked up the brush, inspected it again for loose hairs. "Twenty-nine, 30 ..."

*****

Sandy and Howie met among plenty of shouting and anger — although they were innocent bystanders — neither of them were very far from the action.

It was November 1967, earlier that month the Battle of Dak To became one of the bloodiest battles of the Vietnam War, but it may have only been marginally as bitterly fought as the battle here in the United States between Howie's friend, Marvin, and Sandy's friend, Marilyn.

Marvin had decided to throw himself a birthday party; word quickly got out that there was a party, and the small apartment quickly filled up with friends and friends of friends and complete strangers just looking for a way to pass the night.

Howie had arrived many hours earlier to help Marvin get set up for the party when Sandy and her friend, Marilyn, walked through the open door of the apartment.

Marvin was milling around when he heard the sounds of breaking glass coming from the kitchen. He walked in to find Marilyn shoving pieces of glass with her foot into a pile under the table. He watched as she then emptied the rest of a champagne bottle into huge drinking glasses.

Marilyn had wandered into the kitchen and after rummaging through Marvin's refrigerator, pulled out an expensive bottle of champagne, opened it and poured liberal amounts for herself and her friend Sandy. At least one of the glasses slipped from her hands and broke into several pieces.

Marvin exploded; one word followed another until he loudly demanded that both Marilyn and Sandy get out of his apartment.

Howie watched from the sidelines and as the two women were leaving, he and Sandy started talking. They both would have liked to continue their conversation but Marvin was insistent that Sandy leave and take Marilyn with her. She quickly wrote her telephone number on a slip of paper and handed it to Howie.

Some weeks later, he decided to wear the same sport jacket and found Sandy's phone number in his jacket pocket. He called her and they agreed to go out on a date. It became known as their first official date since neither wanted to mark the start of their relationship with the night of the infamous *champagne heist*.

They went to the Jewel movie theater on Kings Highway in Brooklyn, New York, and saw *Never on Sunday*. After the show, they went to the Foursome Diner on Avenue U, about two and one-quarter miles away. They sat and talked, and talked, and talked, until 2:30 in the morning.

She had heard all the stories about his being a "man about town," or as her friends described him, "a player." But as the evening went on, she found him much deeper than his reputation. He knew about a lot of things and could talk knowledgeably about almost anything. He was pleasant to be with.

He liked her frankness and obvious sincerity. She was bright and articulate and he liked being with her.

Trouble began on their second date. An avid jazz fan, Howie got tickets for a Duke Ellington and Ella Fitzgerald concert. He loved the Duke but really enjoyed listening to Ella Fitzgerald. He counted down the days until the show.

Unfortunately, the one thing he disliked about Sandy was that she was almost always late. He tried really hard to look away, but when it made them late for the Ellington-Fitzgerald concert, it was bordering on the unforgivable.

When he arrived to pick her up there was a note on her door asking him to meet her at the beauty parlor. When he reached the beauty parlor and saw that her hairdresser was still working on her he almost had a fit. But this was just their second date and he did whatever he could to hold back.

They ultimately got to their seats at the concert after Duke Ellington had already been on for a while. They had missed about a quarter of the show which didn't help his mood at all.

As it turned out, even the great Ella Fitzgerald couldn't break them up as a couple. A mutual love and respect was forming. They really cared for and about each other.

Almost eight months after their first date, on Thursday, June 20, 1968, they were married

And that was how it all began.

Both the Jewel movie theater and the Foursome Diner are long since gone, but the marriage between Howie and Sandy lasted for 43 years, until Sandy passed away in 2011.

Sandy's mother was wrong about Howie. He proved to be a successful businessman and a caring and supportive son-in-law and she grew to love and respect him.

M.H.

# The Chair

*The chair is red and yellow. The chair is knee scab red and Spanish onion yellow. The chair is just uncomfortable enough that I never asked to have my turn in it. The chair was her uncle's. The one who lived somewhere in California; we could never quite remember. It was his death gift to her.*

*This chair was her death gift to me.*

We met each other before we even realized. Three different instances where our paths crossed; it was only through our many years together when we finally came to the conclusion we had three other opportunities to meet, which would have been far more interesting than just: I accidentally jabbed her ankles with my cart at the grocery store and after apologizing profusely, she offered me her number and that was that.

Of course, if she were still around to tell this story, she'd be far more detailed and emotional:

"Those lights in grocery stores are so bright, they could teach the blind to see," she'd say. "I was squeezing avocados, making them more ripe by my heavy fondling. I was bent on having one for lunch, two dashes of smoked paprika, sea salt, enough cracked pepper to wake up my nose hairs and a glass of sweet tea." She grew up just outside of Charlotte, N.C., and barely drank anything else.

"I was in an avocado daze when all of a sudden ... SMASH! I could just feel my ankles cave in. I turned around to see this man, rolling out an avalanche of apologies. Well, it hurt like the dickens, but his Sinatra blue eyes made me forget. So, I rattled out a bunch of numbers and told him to call me up like a gentleman and if he was lucky, I might let him take me out on a date."

*The chair is boxy and stern. The chair is a quiet poet dreaming of its next line. The chair still smells like her.*

*It traveled all the way from California to our home in Bangor, Maine. Until now, I never sat in it. Even when she was gone, on various weekend trips with her Mahjong friends or even just running errands, I never sat down there. It was always hers.*

I've spent a lot of time reflecting on the moments, the times we might have met, but didn't. I guess we each needed more time to grow as individuals before we could grow together.

\*\*\*\*\*

The first time we met without meeting, it was a Sunday. I do remember wearing my favorite mustard colored hat, which I wore until the stitching tore its way out. For only the stint of a summer, we had a weekend flea market full of old, and new, and handcrafted, and dug out of garbage cans. She and I could have instantly bonded over our love of antiques, but in a room full of browsers, we somehow found a way to miss each other. Perhaps this was for the best. I was dating a gal named Julah and my (not-yet) wife still had the tear marks scuffing up her cheeks from a recent break-up. So, I guess we were both otherwise occupied.

I was searching through old photographs, which I tend to do. I like touching people's memories like that — all swollen with stillness. If I had seen her, I would have noticed her trying on various hats and shawls. I loved looking at people's memories, while she loved wearing them. To this day, the smell of mildew and mothballs remind me of her, but in a good way. The *best* way.

Julah was with me, and she was completely uninterested. She hated old things and barely liked new ones. I don't think we lasted more than a few months.

I guess it took that long to realize we had nothing in common.

This day stood out because of what happened. In the beginning, the room was just as you'd expect. Pockets of people's wares. There may have been music playing, but I don't remember that. However, I do remember someone screaming *yes, yes*. When I moved closer, I saw it was a woman. And across from her was a man. It seemed he had proposed marriage and luckily, she had accepted. He swooped her up — just like in the movies — and swung her around. The entire room clapped.

Seventeen years into our marriage, we are on a tiny vacation in upstate New York, engaging with the autumn leaves and howls of the moon in a small cabin we had rented for the weekend. The fireplace was crackling with illuminating shades of orange, yellow, and bits of blue. The next morning, we came upon a small flea market in the parking lot of the town library. She mentioned the proposal and the clapping. I gasped. We realized we were amongst the crowd of revelers.

*****

The second time we met without meeting was when I was in the waiting room of my oncologist. I was nervously sweating, losing 15 pounds of my already slim frame just from the anticipation of a possibly devastating diagnosis. All of the available magazines to read were uninteresting — Golf Digest, Fishing Enthusiast, a bunch of fashion magazines. I'm not sure what I would have wanted to read, if offered the choice, but certainly none of those. Each time the person behind the counter called someone's name, my heart jumped inside me like a giant hiccup. I do remember looking around the waiting room to try and distract me, but for some reason she just didn't catch my eye (she hates that part). The overhead TV was playing the news on mute and I tried to guess what tragedies they were announcing based on their facial cues.

One just doesn't forget what happened next. An older man, clearly waiting for a while, fell to the ground and started having a seizure. We all reacted immediately: gasping; lifting his head so he wouldn't bite/swallow his tongue; one woman started fanning his face. We were in a doctor's office, so this was the perfect place to have such a fit. Two doctors emerged and immediately tended to him.

On our one-year anniversary, she and I went to our favorite Indian restaurant, which was actually the only Indian restaurant in our area. We may have been their best customers; in fact, she always joked that we were their only ones. Three years into our relationship, and they wound up closing down.

It was especially quiet that night. My memory recalls that we were the only ones there, but maybe that's not true. As we waited for our order, we chatted away about how quickly that first year had gone, flirtatiously wondering how many more there might be. I later told her that I knew I'd ask her to marry me after our fourth date, maybe even after the first. Though the conversation was flowing, we started to realize that it had been almost 20 minutes without food or even a check-in by the waiter, and usually the service was speedy.

After a significant amount of quiet, I got up to check on our order. When I walked back toward the kitchen, I noticed the chef on the floor. Our waiter was beside her, holding her head.

"Is she OK?" I asked.

"Oh, oh, sorry, she is having a seizure. I called the ambulance. I am so sorry."

I significantly remember that our waiter kept apologizing and then *I* started apologizing because maybe the stress of having to make us food caused this and just a few minutes ago, we were complaining that the service had dropped.

When I got back to the table, I told her what happened and that we should probably go. The ambulance was on its way and would help the chef out.

As we hungrily headed back to her place with a steaming pizza in my backseat from the shop next door, I told her about the other time I witnessed someone having a seizure while waiting on the results of a growth under my arm.

"My goodness," she said. "I experienced the same thing."

We laughed that we could have even been sitting beside each other. She told me how frightened she was that day and I admitted I was too.

Oh, and the tumor was benign.

*The chair indents where her body curved into it. It is like a shadow of her shape. I try not to press too hard with my body; I don't want to alter her impression.*

\*\*\*\*\*

OK, this one is a little more of a stretch, but I want to believe in it entirely.

I was 11 years old and I was in New York City for the first time ever. My family decided we would explore their museums and fit in as many sights as we could in four days. I remember having neck aches, trying to take in the complexity of height from the skyscraping buildings. I just wanted to eat everything and simultaneously not touch anything because, at the time, I felt very uncomfortable by how dirty everything was. Now, I see all that grime as part of the city's many charms.

We were at the Statue of Liberty, which is much bigger up close. As we were traveling there by ferry, I just couldn't fathom how we'd all fit inside. I imagined one person at a time, climbing their way up inside her, taking in the view, and then exiting to make room for another. My mother insisted that many people could fit in. Later, my wife (a devoted Doctor Who fan) referred to the Statue of Liberty as a giant, green Tardis, much bigger on the inside.

Afraid of heights then and now, this was a challenging journey for me. Many stairs and lots of people, all lead me to feel nauseous and dizzy. I'm not sure how far up we were when I lost control of my insides and vomited all over the back of some girl in front of me. If one didn't notice the vomit (unlikely), they would have smelled it immediately. An unpleasant mixture of ingredients that were unrecognizable, yet sour.

"Ew!" she screamed.

The parent of the girl turned around and noticed what had happened. She looked at me with empathy and said something to my parents that I can't remember now. The girl was very upset and yelled at me. I do remember she had hair like summer dandelions and it flowed in uninterrupted waves of curls. I apologized, even though one really has no control over things such as sickness. I think we turned around or maybe we continued. I just remember feeling as green as the Lady's outsides that day.

On the day of our wedding, the air was like the inside of a 400-degree oven. Nothing we could have possibly worn would have given us a reprieve from the heat. We ran out of beverages because everyone just wanted to drink water and sweet tea to quench their microwaved thirst. The food was barely touched because when it is that hot, no one wants to chew or swallow anything.

We were exchanging our vows and afterward, the officiate called up my nephew to hand us our rings. Both of us were so wrapped up in the day, we hadn't noticed that he wasn't himself — usually full of such energy and laughter. As he handed me the ring to put on her, suddenly he lost control and vomited all over me. My sister (his mom) rushed up and profusely apologized.

"Vomiting is a part of life," I said. "And so is love, so let's just keep this going."

My wife chuckled and turned to everyone (only 30 or so friends and family — we preferred to keep it small) and said, "I was about his age when someone vomited on me, so I think this is just part of the cycle of life."

At the time, I didn't think anything of it and the exhilaration of the day led me to forget she had even said anything. It was only just recently, when I started to reflect on these stories, her words, all of our adventures (together and apart) that I remembered that.

So, maybe it was me, and maybe it was her that day inside the Statue of Liberty. And maybe we just weren't meant to meet all those times we almost did.

*The chair is just one object, which reminds me of her. Along with waiting rooms and Indian restaurants and flea markets and New York City and the sky and tall buildings and Fishing Enthusiast magazines.*

A.H.

# What Happens When You Wait

Purchase some seeds. Brown. Eye slits. Like the inside of a musical instrument. Dig into earth with fingers until soil changes the complexion of your nail bed. Throw seeds in.

>Wait.

While you wait, read a book. Gather up a collection of hobbies. Knead bread. Eat bread. Practice how to apologize. Paint a wall your least favorite color. Then, try to fall in love with what you don't understand. Give yourself bangs. Play hopscotch. Burn peanut brittle, but eat it anyway. Write a letter to someone you've forgotten to check in with. Darn your socks. Take a walk and collect as many sidewalk cracks as you can fit into your pocket. Fall in love with the fairy tale of clouds in the sky.

Go visit where your seeds started. Notice what has changed. Kiss the ground as though it has paid you a compliment. Let your toes be tickled by the coolness of dirt and flirtatious earthworms. Do not be afraid of the spiders; they are there to help. Wait some more.

Make yourself a sandwich. Practice how to laugh in various pitches and tones. Learn a new word: hypozeuxis. Start to call yourself this word until your tongue gets twisted and tired. Learn how to play bo-taoshi. Walk barefoot until your feet complain. Forgive your body. Teach yourself 14 words in a new language. Make art. Buy art. Tell an artist how their colors move you. Fall in love with the curvature of commas and semi-colons.

Go back to the home of your seeds. Notice the height of bark and knots.

Count the branches birthed out like limbs. There are leaves now. Greener than the grass stains on your knees. Look up and exercise your neck. Contemplate climbing but decide against it. Measure its shade. How many animals it is now home to. Call it shelter. Call it more than just a tree. Fall in love with what happens when you wait.

A.H.

Aimee Herman and Martin Herman

# The Legalization of Marriage

The next day, after subscribing to every magazine
making 14,000 mix tapes with every ballad from Marvin Gaye to the Supremes
you made a commitment to love.

It was everything they left out in the footnotes and nothing
like the movies.

The food was fried and drippy.
Your tongue sank to the bottom of your throat
from the weight of caloric amusement.

You danced without ever touching the newly reupholstered floors.

Before, you just couldn't believe in Cinderella's paginated declarations.

Now, love wears its copper-dusted promise around your finger.

It always seemed so sour to you, like that forgotten pickle
swallowed by too much vinegar for months.

Until you pressed against that beautifully housed brain
and learned how to believe (again) in believing.

A.H.

Aimee Herman and Martin Herman

# Home
for Trae

seventeen thousand plus five hundred
and forty-four words for you
seven hundred plus ninety-eight
detours
forty-nine Heimlich maneuvers from
fifty-six choking sprees
three hundred plus two hairstyles and
costume changes per year per mood
swing

nineteen thousand plus four shades of
red
ninety-seven miles of gauze to wrap
around the fits of pain
two prescription pads full of side-effects
to well myself for you
thirty stitches and enough scabs to
cover the potholes of memories

forty-seven gallons of spit, eight
pregnancy scares, nineteen break-ins,
one allergic reaction and three wrong
numbers

ninety-one rewrites to get to you
six hundred plus three anxiety attacks
plus four relapses
fourteen tablespoons of terror
one wrong way on a highway meant for
trucks and I am not a truck

thirteen restraining orders and fifteen
plus one-half *un*welcome mats
two small claims courts appearances
and one collision of shyness when you
walked in and wiped the slate of
numbers clean

one hundred and eighty plus
two trees to chop for all the letters
& hoards of stamps
& dedicated postal workers
to stretch words
to get
to find
to reach

you.

A.H.

Aimee Herman and Martin Herman

# No Need for Subtitles

The attraction was instantaneous for him. Years later, he said that the she radiated kindness the first time he saw her.

It took her a bit longer. Her first impression of him was to mentally go through her list of friends and friends of friends and even distant relatives with whom she could pair him with. He was nice and well-mannered and had a charming Old World kind of charm about him. However, he didn't immediately meet her image or definition of *Prince Charming*.

He was working for his uncle, who owned a food and fresh flower store on the east side of Manhattan. He was sweeping the sidewalk outside of the store when he first saw her. The very first thing he noticed about her was her bright red sneakers. As he looked up from the sneakers, he saw a young woman walking hand in hand with a small child on either side of her.

The little girl on the woman's right was arguing, loudly. As they passed, he stared at them, desperately wanting to hear what they were saying even though he knew that all the sounds would be foreign to him. The somewhat out of control noises coming from the little girl were universal. She clearly wanted something that the older, wiser, person in command was not able, or perhaps willing, to permit. What impressed him most was the calm and respectful tone that the young lady seemed to be expressing toward the child. He liked that. He yearned to have such a person to talk to ... to share thoughts with ... to be with.

He had no idea what they were saying, but even in the few seconds of conversation he witnessed as they walked past him, he could clearly see how the child's mood was mellowing as a result of the woman's calm and civil manner.

Each weekday morning, almost exactly at 8 a.m., the three passed his uncle's store; she in her bright red sneakers and the two children. Soon he began timing his sweeping of the sidewalk so as to be outside when they passed.

One day the two children in the care of a different woman came rushing by; similarly the next day and the next. For several hours on the evening of the third day he sat hunched over his Hungarian-English dictionary creating a brief message.

The next morning at around 8 in the morning, he hoped he would see the woman in the red sneakers, but instead he watched as the new woman turned the corner with the two children in tow.

He stepped forward as they were approaching reading aloud from his carefully constructed note, "Does you have information where the lady in the red shoes have gone to?"

The woman seemed startled; she grabbed the children's hands even tighter and rushed past him, avoiding eye contact.

The next morning, he was waiting in front of the store with his broom and his uncle by his side.

His uncle excused himself to the woman as she tried to pass by and said, "Excuse me, we mean you no harm." He pointed to his store. "I own this store and this is my nephew. He was just wondering if you could tell him about the lady with the red shoes. The one he had seen with these two children."

The little boy said, "I think you mean Theresa."

The woman stared down at the child and with tightly clenched teeth said, "We do not speak to strangers." She seemed to have tightened her hold on his hand because the little boy yelped with pain. With the other child in tow, they rushed ahead.

The next morning as they hurried past the store the little boy dropped a crumpled piece of paper. He looked at the man with the broom, put his free hand to his lips and then pointed to the paper. The man waited for them to pass and then picked it up. There were a series of numbers written in crayon.

He took the note to his uncle, told him that it looked like the little boy dropped it for him to read and asked his uncle what he thought it meant.

His uncle put on his reading glasses, looked at what was on the paper, and told his nephew that it looked like a telephone number.

"Whose telephone number?" the man asked.

"Why not dial it and find out?" the uncle responded. "Maybe the woman in red sneakers will be at the other end of this number."

"Can that really be possible?" the man asked in amazement.

"This is America," the uncle said. "Anything is possible. But why guess? Call the number and find out for yourself. What do you have to lose?"

"But I don't speak English," the man argued. "How can I communicate with her?"

"If you want I will call the number for you. I think the little boy is trying to match you two up."

"I don't know," the man said. "If this is her number, I wouldn't want her to be frightened away."

"I don't think the boy would have given you this number if he hadn't already spoken to the woman."

"I don't know," the man said.

"What's to know?"

"I don't know anything about her."

"You know her name, thanks to the little boy, and now you may have her telephone number, again thanks to the little boy. What else do you need to know?"

"I don't know where she lives."

"We'll call ... we'll ask ... if she wants to tell us where she lives, you will know that too. If she doesn't want to tell us where she lives, she won't. You would be no worse off than you are at this very moment. She can't kill you over the phone." The older man gently put his hand on his nephew's shoulder and added, "You are a good man, I will help you in any way I can. Think about it and then decide. There is no need to do anything if you so choose."

Later that day the man said that he thought about what his uncle suggested and decided that he would like his uncle to place the call.

The uncle asked one of his clerks to cover the front of the store and then led his nephew to his office in the back.

The uncle put on his reading glasses and with the piece of paper in front of him, dialed the number. It rang twice and then a woman answered.

"Is this Theresa?" the uncle asked hesitantly.

"No, it isn't. Who is calling?"

The uncle cleared his throat and began to tell the voice at the other end of the line about his nephew and how they came into possession of this telephone number.

The woman said that Theresa was her children's nanny and had fallen and twisted her ankle. While Theresa was recuperating in their home the agency sent a temp to take the children to and from school each day.

The little boy told his mother what had happened when they passed the store and together with her son she talked to Theresa. It was Theresa who suggested they share the telephone number with the man.

She mentioned that the substitute nanny argued against it, and so the boy decided to simply drop it as they passed the store.

After they spoke a little while longer, the woman invited the uncle and his nephew to come to their house the next evening for coffee. She said that it was alright with Theresa and it was also alright with her and her husband.

The next evening, the uncle and his nephew, with a double bouquet of fresh flowers in hand, walked the two blocks from the uncle's store to the address they had been given. They returned again and again, many evenings after that night. The uncle became the translator between his nephew and Theresa.

Theresa never did learn to speak Hungarian, often saying that it was Greek to her. The young man only knew a few words of English and often got their meanings mixed up with parts of other words. However, they soon realized that they both spoke a little German and eventually they worked out some combination of all three languages to communicate without the help of the uncle.

A warm and deep connection soon developed between the two. He became a frequent guest. Some evenings he played checkers with the little boy, while Theresa braided the little girl's hair. As Theresa's foot healed, all four would go for ice cream cones after dinner, or just sit on the steps of the brownstone.

She had never known anyone quite like him. He was sensitive, perceptive and caring.

He loved being with her.

The first time they kissed, was nice, but, as she later confided to one of her friends, no sparks flew; the earth beneath them didn't shake; she wanted a chorus of angels to sing — but none did that night.

Their second kiss didn't happen until several months later.

He had traveled back to Hungary for the wedding of a close cousin and was only gone for nine days, but by the second day she missed him and couldn't wait for him to return.

The day he landed at Kennedy Airport his uncle picked him up and together they went to the brownstone with a ribbon-and-bow-adorned white bakery box. He wanted his uncle to translate for him as he began to tell her the story behind this rich and delicious Hungarian desert — Sütemény Rigo Jancsi.

According to legend, this torte was named after a famous Hungarian gypsy violinist Rigo Jancsi. In 1896 while in Paris, Jancsi played for Prince Joseph and Princess Clara. The princess was instantly attracted to the violinist — it was love at first sight. She left her husband and children to follow Jancsi who divorced his wife. Their affair didn't last very long but the delicious dessert

Rigo created with a confectioner in Clara's honor did.

Later that evening they shared their second kiss.

This time the angel chorus sang.

M.H.

# Frangelico

**1 a.m.**

As I wait for her, the moon harmonizes with my howls. I try not to wonder too loudly what she might be up to, but sometimes I cannot help to dream. Lately, she has been spending more and more time with someone who is not me. This other person looks like her, but is taller. Brown fur on his head. Likes to wear suspenders.

Sometimes the moon is like a circular, glowing treat in the sky. Sometimes it looks like it has been sliced into and is smaller, thinner. I swear, it knows what I am thinking. I tell it my secrets like:

1. My favorite thing about her is how messy she is when she eats. She smiles when I obediently sit beside her, but the truth is I am

just waiting for bits of her food to drop to the floor. Sometimes she swipes it away before I can grab it. Other times, she just lets me have it.
2. I actually don't like her taste in music, but when she sings to me, I can fall into the deepest of sleeps.
3. I've grown increasingly jealous of that thing she opens up and stares at. I can't remember what it's called, but she hits it with her fingers sometimes. It glows, but differently than the moon. I just don't like that it takes her away from me.

Last night, she rubbed my ears and called me her favorite. "My favorite Frangelico," she said. I licked her face and we fell asleep as our dreams wrapped around each other.

## 2 a.m.

When my friend Larry went missing, his human named Penelope put up posters all over the neighborhood with his face on it. I'm not sure what it said, but probably something to do with his absence. He later told me that he got distracted by a squirrel and then met up with Titi, who just gave birth to six and needed some time away from the suckling and yelps. They lost track of time and place, and Larry was too embarrassed by his lack of direction, so he hung out behind the chicken place, where we get our best snacks.

Anyways, maybe I should put her picture on a poster and get them up somehow. She's usually home by now, but maybe she is with *him*. Listen, he isn't so bad. In fact, he sneaks me food when she's not looking, but anything that takes her away from me gets my teeth, you know?

Someone recognized Larry from the posters and got him back home. I didn't see him for a long time after that.

On these late-night talks with the moon, I ask her what it's like to be so far away from us. If she ever gets lonely. She tells me that the stars are extremely talkative and that they even have a book club in the sky, though it's rarely ever poetry, which is her preference to read.

## 3 a.m.

I guess she's not coming home. Who will give her a lick goodnight? Who will bark in her face during an hour she least expects?

Before her, there was someone else; he wasn't as nice. I didn't love him like I love her. He fed me food, which was hard and cold. Nothing fancy like what she feeds me: ice cream and cheese balls and meat gristle and carrots and rice and roast beef and cabbage.

On my birthday (I know this word because she sang it many, many times to me), we took a walk to my favorite place where everyone seems to know my name and loves me almost like she does. They crouched down and pet me, kissed my head, and showed me their teeth. She taught me that this is called a smile. They always smile at me. She told me I could choose any kind but chocolate. I know this word because I can never have it. Bad for me, she says. Dangerous.

I chose the white kind and they put it in a little dish and placed on the floor beside me. Everyone watched as I lapped up this delicious, cold treat. Ice-cream, it's called. I know this because it is my favorite. And then everyone else sang the song with *birthday* in it. I felt like I was the best one.

She makes me feel this way every day.

**7 a.m.**

I must have fallen asleep because the moon has lost its glow, but I can still see it dimly shining up there. I look around and she's still not here. My food dish is empty, but I have water.

When I first met Larry, we shared stories about our humans. Kind of like a comparison of who was better. His human has a bigger house, but mine has a bigger heart.

I won.

**7:23 a.m.**

"Frangelico!!!!!!!!!!!!!!!!!!!"

I hear her keys curl into the door, right before it opens. She runs toward me and gives me more kisses than I can count. It's too much and I love it.

"I fell asleep at Trae's, and didn't realize how much time had passed. Could you ever forgive me?"

I rolled onto my belly (favorite position) and she began to scratch me. I smiled in the only way that I know how (from within).

"Frangie, Trae and I were talking and we've decided to move in together. What do you think about that?"

"..."

"The thing is, I really love him."

*Love?*

"But, of course, I will always love you most. With every ounce of my heart. You know this, right?"

"..."

"You think there is room for one more?"

One of the reasons Larry got extra caught up by that squirrel (besides the obvious) is that he was a little distraught (I'm not sure how I know this word) because his human had also just let another into their home. Larry did not like her. I told Larry to give her a chance and that if this new human makes *his* human happy, that is all that matters. I tried to remember this as *my* human was talking to me.

I thought about how my human felt before she met Trae. Water dripped out of her face all the time. She barely ate, which meant I lost out on all the special treats she'd give to me. She could barely get up to walk me — though she never forgot my needs.

I don't have the kinds of words she has, so I licked her until she lost herself in laughter.

"I guess that's a yes! Yes! I love you, Frangie. OK ... let's have some breakfast and search out the language of the sun today. Then we can put on some music, have a dance party — just you and I — and make room for a new member of our family."

A.H.

Aimee Herman and Martin Herman

# Hibernation

In the wintertime, it is just a little too difficult to fall in love. We are dressed like houses: heavily insulated, curtains closed, with not even a hint of skin showing. We walk around with red, dripping noses and dry, flattened hair, hurrying from one heated shelter to another. The sky drops hints of flirtations, uniquely shaped snowflakes gracefully plunging from the sky, dotting lips and shoulders, but we are often too shivery to notice.

The days are like blinks, offering such minimal sunlight before the ceiling above us grows frail and ominous. The trees are nudists; their leaves left behind as the branches grow thin and crackled. And the streets grow an off-white moss over pavement from the lingering shadows of snowfall. The sun is a memory.

It is the abdomen of winter: the beginning of February. My neighbors believe the worst is behind us, but I remain unsure of this, with swollen windows, quivering from the cold to keep me company. Everything I could possibly love exists out there. Outside. The haunt of summer skin, shimmering from slow-motion sunburn, is like a song playing in a room too vast to sing along to.

So I sit like Virginia Woolf may have, or Emily Dickinson, writing and gazing, imagining the frozen life that lingers just outside my warmth. I hunch over notebook or computer skin, with legs wrapped in blankets, drinking enough mugs of hot cocoa to render me a moustache of steamed brown foam above my lip, but I leave it there. I am alone, but there are enough sounds in here to keep me company: the whirr of a half-empty refrigerator, the cars outside sliding over ice, the birds too lazy to have planned ahead, and the airplanes too high to hitch a ride on.

In the morning, my routine is anything but enthralling. I slowly press myself out of bed, and go on small pilgrimages to the kitchen to boil water for coffee. Everything seems further away in the winter, so I call it a trek, though if I counted all my steps — and I have: 13 — I might really just call it a few lonely hops.

In these months of wool and slumber, my skin is a chalkboard. I write out grocery lists and love letters to no one on my dry, cracked flesh. *This* is romantic. Epistolary conversations on my thighs and arms, knees and belly, about the day I am having or will have.

Love is funny in that way. It can be completely encapsulated within the mind of a quirky writer during the darkest days of the year, to her skin.

On an otherwise nondescript Thursday, a poet comes to visit me. His name is Baudelaire and we sit on my couch as he reads to me in French about all the ways he has wandered. For lunch, I make sandwiches wearing homemade blackberry jam. Baudelaire tells me that he would climb to this elevated railroad in a city too busy to have a name, and watch people.

He told me that for these hours he would fall in love with strangers because he felt like a momentary part of their lives. He observed couples fighting and children having fits. He watched a woman cry into a handkerchief until it seemed like there was no salt left, and then she just began to laugh. He memorized the way her mouth went from droop to stretch in minutes. I told him that I always want to be in love before winter begins, so I have someone to huddle against. I told him that once that first drop of cold begins, love hides in caves.

This is when Baudelaire put down his sandwich and grabbed my hand. I let him because we were in my home and it was lunchtime and I was curious about why he wanted to take my skin in his.

"Have you ever listened to 'Blue in Green'" he asked.

"What do you mean? The sound of a color trapped inside a color?"

"No, the song. By Miles Davis," he answered.

"I haven't." I was too ashamed to admit I rarely listened to music at all these days as it fed upon so many of my despondencies.

This is when Baudelaire grabbed something from his pocket. It looked like a miniature record player. And when he pulled it all the way out, it grew in size. Out of his bag, he pulled out a record. I could barely swallow the slightly stale bread with sweet jam because it grew stunned in my mouth.

"Where ... how did you ...?" I could barely speak.

"Don't worry about that," he said. "I want to play you this song."

We listened in silence to the slowly spinning record.

"Tell me what you feel," Baudelaire prodded.

"I feel ... warm. Hungry, but ... also like I ate every food that ever made me feel satiated, all at once, but without overwhelm or overstuff. I feel ... light and a little turned on. I feel ... love."

Baudelaire smiled and we sat together like this, listening to Miles in the warmth of my living room in winter when I never expected I could feel this way. This type of *feeling*, of being alive and alert and well, in love.

A.H.

# Shelly and Greg: An Almost Love Story

Greg ran down the stairs and into the subway car. He made it just as the doors were closing. It was well past rush hour so he had no problem finding a seat.

As his breathing returned to normal, he glanced around and locked eyes with a young woman, about half a car length away. *Where do I know her from,* he thought Finally, he got up and walked over to her, "Excuse me, I know you, but I can't seem to put a name with your face. May I sit down here?" He pointed to an empty seat opposite her.

"You paid the same exorbitant fare I did to get on this train, sit wherever you want," she said.

"Honestly, this is not a come on but you do look familiar," he said.

"Maybe I should open my blouse to nudge your memory," she sneered.

"I really am not trying to pick you up. Do we know each other?" he persisted.

"Yes."

"You aren't going to make this easy for me, are you?" he said.

"I don't make things easy for anyone, anymore."

They sat in silence for a while. He moved forward, beginning to get up to return to his first seat and then it hit him. "Sherry, that's it, your name is Sherry."

"It's Shelly, but I guess that is close enough."

"Yes, Shelly, that's your name."

"Give the little man a prize," she said.

"How are you?" he said.

"Terrific. But don't get any ideas; I'm not the same person you now remember."

"We all change; I am not the guy you knew back then either. What has it been, four years?" he asked.

"Something like that."

"Well, how are you doing?" he asked.

"What is this, a neighborhood reunion?" she asked, staring coldly in the opposite direction.

"Any chance we can restart this conversation? Hi! How are you?"

"We did that already, in fact, if I remember correctly, we did everything already," she said.

"Well, not quite everything."

"Let me see, I was 13 and you were, what, 30?" she said.

"I was 17."

"Oh, I guess that makes it alright," she said.

"Look, I might have been a few years older than you but believe me, I was far from a 'man of the world' and I apologize. But ... all we did was kiss."

"You kissed a 13-year-old and you were 17. Actually, that was plenty," she said.

He started to get up, and she put her hands up to stop him.

"I'm sorry, you are trying to be nice and I am just unloading on you because I had a crappy day. Yes, let's start over. Hi! I am Shelly and yes I remember you, Greg."

He sat down again. "And how have you been?" he asked.

"I've survived," she said.

"Still living in the Coney Island Houses?"

"My parents still live there so I guess I do too ... with my 3-year-old daughter." She smiled. "Isn't this the place in the conversation when you are supposed to say, 'this is my stop,' and get off the train as quickly as you can?"

"So ... you're married?"

"No."

"Divorced?"

"No."

"Separated?"

"I guess you could say that, although we were never *really* together in any recognized form."

"The child's father isn't in the picture now?" he asked.

"He was all over me until I told him I was pregnant. Then he forgot where I lived. Actually, his mother sent him off to live with some far off relative. He's never been in my daughter's life. What do you care? What are you ... writing a book?"

"I thought you agreed to start over?" he said.

She turned her head towards him and said, "You're right. Her name is Jennifer."

"That's a nice name."

"She's terrific. I would have preferred to have her come along when I was older than 15, or at a more convenient time, but now that she is here, I wouldn't trade her for anything. She is the best thing in my life."

"Say, I get off at New Utrecht Avenue. My car is by the station, would you like to get off at my stop so we can have coffee? I would be happy to drive you home."

"I told you, I'm not the same person you remember."

"I was not trying to come on to you," he said.

"I'm sorry," she said. "You just picked a bad day to renew old acquaintances."

"Okay, baby steps, may I call you?"

"For what purpose," she asked.

"Does there have to be a purpose other than to talk like two human beings?" he asked.

"I don't give my phone number out so quickly, anymore."

"Then I won't give you my phone number."

"I didn't *ask* for your phone number," she said.

"I know, and it is killing me."

She laughed.

"Gee whiz, she can laugh, well, that is definitely a start," he said.

"Let's say I give you my phone number. You will never call and we both know it."

"Now, why would I ask for it if I had no intention of following up?" he said.

She opened her purse and pulled out a pen and a small notepad. She wrote a series of numbers on one of the pages along with her name.

"Here ... if a man answers, it will be my father. And if I tell him how we first met, he will probably throw you out of the nearest window."

He laughed.

"How about dinner this Saturday night," he asked as he took the paper from her.

"I like to spend Saturday night with my daughter."

"Then let's make it lunch on Saturday and you can bring your daughter as our chaperone."

"At 3 years of age, she wouldn't make a very good chaperone. Plus, I don't think it is such a good idea to introduce her to a lot of strange men in my life."

They sat quietly as the train came into a station. When the doors closed and the train began to enter into the dark tunnel she said, "I guess lunch on Saturday would be alright."

*****

He hesitated for a few minutes, nervously excited, and then knocked on the door. It opened and an older version of Shelly appeared.

"Hi! I'm Greg. I came to take Shelly to lunch."

"I know who you are and why you are here. Your mother owned the grocery store across the street a while back."

"Guilty as charged," he said.

"I guess you can come in." The woman turned and yelled into the apartment, "Shelly, someone is here to see you."

She was wearing a simple dress and a scarf covered in yellow happy faces.

He stared and with a half-smile said, "I remember that scarf."

"You should."

"I can't believe you still have it."

She blushed. She was hoping he would notice.

"You pulled it out for today's date?"

"This isn't a date — it is just a lunch. Let's be clear about that."

*****

As soon as he pulled into the parking space, she jumped out of the car. They walked toward the ball field. Several old men were playing chess on a long picnic table. It was chilly for a June afternoon, and when he saw her shiver, he took off his jacket and put it around her shoulders. At first, she protested but she was cold and wrapped the jacket tightly around herself.

He was the first to speak, "Do you work in the city?"

"Yes, if you can call it work."

"What do you do?"

"I answer phones for an ad agency."

"I would call that work."

"I guess. It pays the bills. When it became clear that my growing midsection wasn't just from too many desserts, they made me leave school. There aren't very many jobs for someone without much of a formal education, so I guess I should be happy I have a job."

"You could go back to school now."

She glared at him.

"There is always night school."

"Hey, it is what it is; and it *isn't* any of your concern."

He stopped walking and put his hands firmly onto her shoulders. "How about a truce for today. Just two adults walking, talking and eventually having lunch?"

"Okay, truce," she said, holding up her hands in mock surrender.

"So, have you considered going back to school? It could be really—"

"I thought about it. In fact, I think about it all the time, but I was never a great student and the thought of going back and failing at one more thing in my life isn't all that appealing."

They were coming to a small café. He pointed toward it and reached ahead to open the door for her.

After they were seated, a waitress handed them each a menu.

He said, "Does anything appeal to you?"

She pointed to one of the sandwiches and when the waitress arrived, he ordered two of the same.

"And a cup of coffee, please," she added.

"Two," he said.

After a long and uncomfortable silence, she asked, "So, what do you do?"

"I work in an office days and go to Brooklyn College at night."

"What are you taking up?"

"Space."

She laughed.

"Is there a *master plan*?"

"I'm just taking it a day at a time."

"Sounds to me like neither of us are on a winning track," she said.

He nodded.

*****

They went out one more time, a week or so later.

He called her a few times after that, left messages with her mother, but she chose not to return his calls.

They saw each other on the subway a few more times. He nodded to her and she smiled back but neither chose to move closer.

Then there was the night when the subway car suddenly went dark.

He had just entered the subway car, and noticed her wearing the scarf with yellow happy faces, sitting in her regular seat. He smiled and as he reached his seat, the lights went out.

No one panicked or moved. Fairly quickly, two policemen entered their car announcing that there had been a small trash fire further down the track. As a precaution, the power was cut off. One of the policemen forced open the car door and led the passengers in a single file back to the nearest station where city buses were made available.

He walked over to her and suggested that they share a taxi when they get back up to the street level. She hesitated, and then finally agreed.

He gave the driver her address. When they reached her building, he got out of the taxi and walked around to her side of the car. He told her that he would like to see her again.

She said it wasn't a good idea. He said he understood.

She reached into her purse to pay the taxi driver. He told her he would take care of it when the taxi dropped him off at his apartment. She insisted on paying, handed the driver a 20-dollar bill, said a quick goodbye and walked toward the front door of her building.

He watched until she was inside, and then got back into the taxi and went home.

That was the last time he ever saw her.

\*\*\*\*\*

When she got home, she quickly looked in on her daughter and then went into her room and closed the door. The scarf felt heavy around her neck. She took it off and noticed the tissue paper, which she had kept it in all these years. It was faded pink. She spread out the paper and lovingly placed the scarf in the center. Slowly and gently, she folded the outer edges of the paper inward, knowing this would be the last time she would ever wear it. Every now and then, when she was alone in the apartment, she took the scarf out of its pink wrapping, spread it out across her bed and thought about what might have been.

M.H.

# First Date

**1.**

You brush your teeth three times with five minutes in between each session out of fear that you missed one. You scrub away last night's leftovers of two-day old Indian food — cumin and cardamom particles crushed between teeth. You remove remnants of your morning's cup of coffee and the one you desperately needed this afternoon. The slightly stale peanut butter sandwich. The shot of rum you had to drink after brushing number two to slur away your nerves. You never forget your tongue.

**2.**

You met her through a dating app for book lovers. You met him in the grocery aisle beside the organic flours; he was shopping, you were lost. You met her in a chat room for hypoglycemics. You met him at the library, which you ducked into for the high-powered air-conditioning; he was in search of *War and Peace* in large print. You met him through the friend of your ex-friend. You met her at the movies: several seats between you while watching a resurrected print of *Harold and Maude*. You met her in AA. You met him at the DMV. You met on a Tuesday in the parking lot at the mall, while briefly fighting over the same spot.

## 3.

Your grooming began three days ago. Steamed open skin, massaged pores, tried to scrub some of your age away. You used that aftershave your fancy shmancy brother gave to you, which he promised would lure in the ladies. You shaved your legs; you shaved your face. You loofah'd the calluses off your toes because you never know where a first date might lead. You plucked that lone hair which has grown attached to your chin. You lotioned the dryness away from your elbows. You got a manicure, a pedicure, you soaked the tired off your feet. You tried out three new colognes — one of which was featured as a sample in your now-expired magazine subscription. You thought about getting your ear pierced to make you appear tough. You try on all your jewelry. You decide not to wear a tie this time.

## 4.

Your mother calls and you immediately regret telling her. She wants to know their occupation (how are *you* to know?). She wants a description; you tell her pictures aren't always reliable. She begins to laugh and you recognize this as her giddiness toward future grandbabies. She tells you she drank two espressos to keep her awake, so she could hear all the details. You tell her you'll call her in the morning. You forget.

## 5.

You map out directions toward at least 15 possible conversation topics. You practice four variations of your laughter. You stare at your reflection for almost an hour because you've been told you are horrible at eye contact. You try to remember all the reasons someone might want to fall in love with you.

## 6.

You take a taxi to her house because your car broke down because you don't want her to know that your windshield looks like a shooting star exploded against it because no one ever taught you how to fix a flat. When he arrives at your house, he is carrying flowers you recognize from your neighbor's backyard. You invite her in for a drink beforehand, and learn you have been mispronouncing her name. You both decide to meet at the restaurant and you arrive early enough to sweat right through your shirt; you do your best to casually flap your arms to air yourself out. You realize, while riding on the bus, that you have a massive unidentifiable stain on the front of your shirt. You realize you are covered in cat hair dog hair bird feathers. You get lost on your way to the movie theater and miss the previews; you practically fall in her lap trying to find her in the dark. You only realize later that you had some bright memory of lunch lodged between your two front teeth. You are 43 minutes late because of traffic, an anxiety attack, a wardrobe malfunction.

## 7.

You never know which fork to use but that seems to charm him. When she talks about her ex, you practice all the different ways you can appear as though you are paying attention. You both order the same thing, but yours is undercooked; you are too shy to say anything. He laughs at all your jokes. You bond over a love of algebra and *Murder She Wrote*. You run out of things to talk about during minute 12. You cannot read the menu because you look so much better without glasses. He chokes during the appetizer but you win him over with your Heimlich. She calls your smile *musical*. You worry he is more interested in the waitress. You realize you may be not-so-distantly related, so you end it before the entrée arrives. You are charmed when she orders dessert first. You forget to mention your allergy to shellfish. He starts to serenade you. She talks more about her mother than herself. You start to feel like a city on fire from all the spice and he asks you why your face is so red. She kisses your hand and you like it. Your lips swell the size of Montana and you never see him again.

## 8.

He invites you back to his place where you spend the rest of the night playing *Super Mario Kart*. He asks you permission to kiss you, but doesn't wait for your answer. You realize you live in the same building, which makes it awkward when you make your way home. She offers to fix you dessert and you sit on her couch as she whips up tres leches. You invite him over to watch *Annie Hall* but you don't make it past the opening credits. When she kisses you, your body feels reborn. When he opens his apartment door, you are greeted by the scent of four hundred cats, yet he only seems to own one. She explains that she used to have furniture before the "bed bug incident." He tells you that he's been having housing issues and inquires if you're interested in a roommate. Each time he touches you, you think about marriage. She falls asleep beside you and the sound of her snores is your new favorite song.

A.H.

# The lovely Lora ...

I wish to begin by telling you that I love Lora Chan.

I love her passion for life and people and fashion and music and the way she makes me feel every time she walks into the room.

I love the way she can cut through everyday nonsense and shine her honesty on the who, the what, and why of most any topic.

I share her super-sized appreciation for shrimp with lobster sauce and really good pizza and movies and popcorn and clutter around her computer keyboard, and the sweet smell of fresh flowers and my home made stewed mushroom omelet.

I have learned to enjoy coffee ice cream because it is her favorite flavor.

I may never understand her fondness for shoes, closets full of shoes, plus more shoes in piles left here and there.

We were born in two very different exotic and possibly even strange places — she in Hong Kong, me in Brooklyn, New York.

We are of different religions and political persuasions, but each thoroughly committed to the other.

For us, love came later in life. I think that is a good thing. With age comes a greater understanding of what makes for a caring and supportive partner. With the mellowness of age comes a solid understanding of, and a deep appreciation for, the pleasure of just sharing a breakfast or lunch or dinner — of looking into her eyes ... of hearing about the news of her day, good or bad.

With maturity, even waiting for the Triple A truck to recharge your battery, (which died because I left the lights on), becomes a pleasant excuse to just sit together and chat.

For almost a decade before I met Lora, I lived alone — except for my daughter's two cats. As a result, I was a real challenge for Lora. The first time we went out to dinner, she had to do all the talking just to break the deafening silences. It had been a long time since I was in a social setting with a woman and it showed. I thank God every day that she hung in until I learned how to trust again.

When Juliette the cat developed cancer, it was Lora who tenderly but effectively gave Juliette her daily morphine injections. (I held Juliette, but I don't think I ever could have handled it without Lora.)

Yes, there have been differing points of view and even a few arguments; but never a reason to mistrust or dislike or un-love this very special woman.

I began this narrative by saying that I love Lora. I would like to end this narrative by saying that I love Lora.

M.H.

# Schadenfreude

Nyman Rifling and Renita Goils ate dinner together on a Wednesday during happy hour prices at a restaurant with a **B** grade written on the front window, when the weather outside was neither pleasant nor stormy.

Nyman could be called fat, but more specifically Mr. Rifling is far more obese than spaciously curved. In fact, he found most doctors judgmental of the status of his skin, so he stopped attending all medical appointments of any kind about 14 years ago. You will assume he is an over-eater, but he is far more than just that. He sees food like music that he not only listens to, but digests all day, dancing to the rhythm of each crunch, swallow, slurp, and burp.

Nyman lives in an apartment building that reminds him of a two-week old croissant: crumbly, stale, and far past its expiration date. But he loves his apartment for one single reason: he lives below the beautiful, magnificent, utterly stimulating presence of Renita Goils. As corpulent and globular as Nyman is, Renita is quite the opposite. She is like a paper doll, barely imprinting the ground as she walks. Nyman is a six-piece sectional couch, while Renita is simply an ottoman — dainty, taking up the tiniest bit of space.

How odd a pairing. But you see, so often we desire what we aren't. Or what we'd like to be. Nyman has lived in this rancid pastry of a building for more than two decades. Renita moved in just seven months ago, but Nyman has been aware of her existence since she first moved in, accompanied by three men and one burly woman loading in her many boxes of stuff. He thought about baking her a pie or casserole or batch of cornmeal muffins, but each time he took a gift for her out of his well-used oven, he'd gobble it up, unable to commit to letting his food go.

Then, a few weeks after Renita's arrival, the most wonderful thing happened to Nyman: the postal worker accidentally left a piece of mail meant for Renita Goils in his mailbox. Thus, this became the perfect excuse to meet her.

It was a Sunday, Renita's favorite day of the week, though Nyman did not know this. Renita liked to read the police blotter section in the local newspaper, which came out on this day. She reveled in others getting caught and the often, careless reasons that led them toward police custody. Don't mistake Renita for an unkind person; she is actually quite thoughtful. But early in life she developed a thirst for other's misfortune, which was bizarrely connected to her libido. That is to say, Sunday was the day Renita Goils masturbated and *this* was her way of getting off.

Nyman Rifling gathered his greasy hair toward the right side of his head. It was thin, like a collection of dead spider legs, stretched out, buried against his forehead. He often just left his hair alone, but today he would be delivering Renita's mail to her and he wanted to look his best. He searched through his armoire for the right shirt to wear — one with little to no stains, inclusive of all buttons, breast pocket sewed on completely and not dangling like a suicide jumper off a rooftop.

Mr. Rifling looked OK. *Just OK*, which was far better than any other day, so one might even say that Nyman Rifling looked his best.

In today's Sunday police blotter, Renita Goils read about a man one county away who got caught stealing several tubes of hemorrhoid cream from a local pharmacy that sold that sort of thing. He not only stuck them into his pockets, but threw them down his pants as well.

According to the written news report, this unfortunate man began leaving a trail of tubes as he tried to slyly slink out the door.

*Like breadcrumbs for his anus*, Renita thought, smiling through her thin, yet glossy lips. This not only amused her greatly, but in fact, she found herself getting extremely turned on. Ms. Goils brought her tiny fingers — called toothpicks by a man she once had relations with years ago — and led them underneath her loose dress to feel just how aroused she was. Renita's moans sounded almost like tiny laughs. A gurgle of giggles drifting out of her mouth.

She first learned how to masturbate from an instructional video addressed to the previous tenant, which she almost threw away. Then, she gave into temptation, and opened up the cardboard packaging. She noted her kindled loins from the knowledge that *someone* hoping to learn how to "touch themselves toward maximum pleasure" would be lost forever. Once again, Renita Goils is not a masochist. Unfortunately, others' tragedy is her only way to pleasure.

Renita was moments away from *her* maximum pleasure when she heard a knock at the door. Or to be more precise, a pounding. The knuckles against her painted wood door sounded like a cavalcade of festival goers ground up into one massive fist. She frustratingly pushed her dress back down, smoothed it out with her damp fingers and licked them clean. You must know, Ms. Goils was raised with the utmost of manners and would never leave a person waiting.

"Oh, hello," Renita said, after opening the door and noting the latitude of Mr. Rifling.

Renita did not know this, but Nyman had practiced for quite a long time the words he would say at this very moment. However, it was also in this moment, which he had forgotten every single one of those rehearsed words.

"Are ... are you OK?" Renita inquired after an unpleasant amount of silence.

"Yes, I ... your mail." Nyman reached into his pocket and lifted out the envelope addressed to the most beautiful name he had ever read. Several crumbs from what may have been crushed cornflakes also came out of his pocket.

"Thank you," Renita spoke, grabbing the letter covered in bits of food and sweat from Nyman's nervous threads. "You are—"

"I'm Nyman Rifling, apartment 4B, just below you, in fact."

"Would you ... like to come in?"

Nyman has been alive for exactly 46 years, eight months and 14 and a half days. And yet, it was not until this very moment that he had ever heard more wonderful words jump against his earlobe, tickling his insides.

"Yes!" he uttered far too excitedly.

Nyman Rifling and Renita Goils sat together on her green and yellow striped couch with impressively supple springs beneath the slightly beat-up cushions, and talked like two strangers often do. Covering such topics as: the weather ("A bit cold, but not *too*," decided Renita); books ("Yes, I've read some," declared Nyman); and ways to spend a rainy day ("Beneath a roof which does not leak," said Renita).

After almost 20 minutes, Renita gasped.

"I did not offer you anything to eat," she said. "Are you ..." Here, is where Ms. Goils's voice trailed as she dripped her sight from top to bottom, noting Nyman's size once again. "... hungry?"

"Always," Nyman admitted, without shame or hesitation. "I would love to cook for you sometime," he said.

Renita smiled and said yes, but then, "How about tonight?"

"Oh!" Nyman gasped. "Well, I'd ... I'd have to go grocery shopping first, and out of respect, plan a menu of deserving proportions and—"

Renita interrupted Nyman without apology and suggested they go out to dinner. "Less dishes to worry about cleaning," she announced. "And anyway, then you won't have to go to any trouble. How about Salvatore's? If you like Italian, of course."

It would be inaccurate for Nyman to admit to any restrictions to his eating regime. In fact, he desired all food, though happened to be severely allergic to fennel. But he didn't really consider that food worth mentioning anyway.

So it was on that particular Sunday that Mr. Rifling and Ms. Goils walked over to Salvatore's pizzeria, just a few streets away from their apartment building for their first date.

Nyman was at his best, which you must know by now is not too far from his worst. And Renita looked like a polished vase, slender and demure, hair brushed so that each strand remained like soldiers in line, no piece out of place.

You've been on enough dates to know what happens next: various forms of fidgeting, a spill of some sort, two separate trips to the bathroom, nervous bouts of silence, laughter during moments which did not call for such, and the inevitable sex talk.

"I realized when I first watched the Jerry Springer show for 20 minutes or so," Renita spoke.

"I ... I'm not familiar with—"

"It's not like I'm expecting to learn anything from these silly shows," Renita interrupted. "I just ... well, if you must know, I really like seeing others whose lives are just complete and utter messes. I wait for the punching to happen. And they are *always* ready for it with security guards on the side of the stage. You know, Nyman ..." Renita paused, "I hope you do not find this unappealing, but when blood is drawn or hair pieces are pulled out, I grow quite aroused."

It is necessary to announce that Renita had consumed two and three-quarters glasses of house red wine during the course of this dinner, to which she had only eaten four to 12 strands of spaghetti, three green beans and two bites of an impressively stale dinner roll.

There was a stain of merlot just above and below her lips, creating a clown-like spread of red on her pale skin. If she were aware of it, she'd be mortified. However, across the table, Nyman was quite turned on.

"Schadenfreude," Nyman said, with bits of spinach ricotta ravioli still clinging to the various spaces between his teeth.

"I don't ... understand," Renita whispered.

"It's German. To ... take pleasure in other's misfortune."

Renita grabbed the red scratchy linen napkin from her lap and, with pure grace, dotted her lips. "I'm not mean, I just—"

"Oh, no," Nyman quickly interrupted. "I would never ... I would never think that of you. Actually, I find it charming. *You*, I mean. I find *you* charming."

When dinner was over, Nyman and Renita left quite aware of what was to come next. Nyman's belly protruded further than it had upon entering the Italian eatery, having finished not only his meal and two helpings of dinner rolls, but Renita's meal as well.

They walked the several streets back to their shared building, Nyman's fingers wrapped completely around Renita's. She felt safe around Nyman and quite liked his size. She'd never met anyone as large as him, yet he seemed to be so comfortable and unapologetic about his massive girth.

Nyman Rifling walked Renita Goils to her front door, hoping to at least get a good night kiss. He was unpracticed and nervous, but excited to feel Renita's lips press against his. He was not prepared for her bony arms to grab him, as she lifted her height at least one more inch on tiptoes.

Then, she whispered toward his ears, "I've got one-day-left-before-expiration-date cookies in my cupboard. And this video you might like to watch with me. Would you like to come inside?"

A.H.

# Dragonflies

When I was young, imaginations weren't required to be plugged in. There was no need for AAA batteries, or a reliable wireless connection to pretend myself into a variety of situations. I could be a pirate, or a police officer, or a war hero, or an archeologist, all in the span of moments, depending upon how I was feeling that day. This is why Zeya and I got on so well. She hated dolls and board games and even television. She hated anything that took away her ability to make things up. So, we would cut out photographs of people from my mother's fashion magazines and create our own paper dolls. And we'd make up rules to made-up games and we even wrote a play that (we felt) was far better than anything on television or movie screens. Zeya and I could be forced into a dark room with nothing but walls and wood and we'd never run out of things to do or talk about. Needless to say, she was my best friend.

We were 11 or maybe 12, old enough to be allowed to roam freely in the mall without parental supervision. I waited for this privilege for an extremely long time. Just like my sister, Shiri, waited to be able to wear make-up and then go out with boys. I didn't care about any of that stuff; even now, more than 30 years later, I still don't.

"Let's be middle-aged ladies without husbands or babies," Zeya said while we were in the boy's section of our favorite clothing store at the mall. My memory is almost impeccable; I could remember the weather that day too, if I thought you cared enough.

"Who spend our days researching unclaimed species in the rainforest," I added. "And by night, we live in a cabin on the top of a secluded mountain. We use rainwater to hydrate us and dumpster dive for our supper. We'll live together, of course. And I will be extra good at finding really delicious garbage food, because I'll know exactly which ones to rummage in, but you will be best at turning my trash treasures into a meal!"

Zeya just smiled at me. "Yeah, and we wouldn't care about what we wore or stupid fads that just separated people from each other because we'd be living science out loud!"

"Do you like this?" I held a shirt up and pressed it against me. It was blue. Striped. Pristine with buttons and price tag.

"Yeah, you gonna try it on?"

"I, uh, no, I just—"

Zeya looked at me and grabbed my hand, squeezing it tightly. "You simply *must* try it on. Tonight we are celebrating because you just discovered a new breed of ... of ..."

"Dragonfly!" I screamed.

"Yes! Dragonfly! And Helen, our boss, has promoted you to ... head researcher, and so we have that party tonight to celebrate!"

I looked at Zeya and could feel all of my teeth exposed from the width of my smile.

We never really talked out loud about our shopping mall destinations. We always just gravitated toward the same places: Cindy's Cinnamon Buns (Zeya's mom's were gluten and sugar-free, so when we went out, she liked to let loose and eat all the foods forbidden in her house), Lids (hat shop), the candy shop that always had the best free samples, and Cards & Things (because we loved reading the cards and looking at the things).

Zaya loved trying on clothes and pretending to be different people each time she changed. When I first led Zaya toward the boy's side, she didn't even inquire why or laugh at me for liking boy's clothes. It's like she just knew or something.

"So, you're going to try it on, right?"

I never tried anything on. That would mean going into a dressing room, and I always assumed it was for boys only. Boys who looked like boys and were *called* boys, but I was a ... a ... *Jennifer*.

"No, I—"

"C'mon, J. It's cool. I'll go in with you."

So, on the day we pretended I had discovered a new species of dragonflies and was being honored, therefore needing something new to wear, I found myself trying on this blue, collared *boy's* shirt. And I remember this day because it was the day I felt like all my skin was suddenly alive. It's like when my parents got rid of that crummy mustard yellow couch that we had since I was born. We had flipped the cushions so many times; all the stains had just created some sort of pattern, like an upholstered Picasso, if he had ever ventured into furnishings. And when you sat on it, you could feel the springs digging into you. It was terrible. Then one day, I came home from school and there was this new couch. It was brown like a giant milk chocolate candy bar, but fuzzy with thick pillows and when you sat down, all you felt was extreme coziness. Everyone who sat on that couch fell asleep. *Mount Couchmore*, my uncle Harris called it. Anyway, this is how I felt in that shirt. Not sleepy, but cozy. Like my skin was finally pressed against the right fabric. Or like every other shirt I had ever worn spoke a language I just couldn't understand, and this one shared my exact secret vocabulary.

Of course, I bought the shirt.

I wound up collecting far more shirts and neither of my parents ever noticed. Or they certainly didn't say anything. Maybe they saw how happier I was wearing clothes that made me feel more me than I ever felt before.

Zeya and I are still friends, but living on separate coasts now. She's not quite a middle-aged lady, and almost true to her imaginings, no husband, but she adopted a baby a few years ago. I mentioned that day to her and she remembered it just as loudly as I did.

"Yes!" she said. "The day you discovered a new kind of dragonfly and you discovered another part of you."

A.H.

Aimee Herman and Martin Herman

# Norma Jean

I grab a countlessly folded dollar bill from my wallet and place it into my front pocket. It kind of looks like a love note, faded green with secret fibers and tiny lettering, but to some it is even more coveted than love because it is money.

"Love can't solve my overdue electric bill," my friend Gina recently said to me. "I can't give my landlord a pile of love and call it my rent. Or maybe I can," she said. "He's kinda strange. But I sure as hell don't want to find out."

It is 14 minutes past seven in the morning, late enough that the garbage trucks have already collected our trash. Empty cans now litter the sidewalks with the smells of what once existed inside them ghosting the air.

My dog has been walked. Teeth are brushed. Got my work outfit on, which is really no different from my *off* clothes. Drank enough coffee to wake the words up, sleeping in my throat all night.

I never know if she is going to be there. For the first few months, I didn't know her name. She would give her smile to me: bright white, uniformed (possibly no longer hers), and tentative; I would give her a dollar.

Finally, on a random Wednesday when the early morning air had a slight breeze to it — not quite kite-flying weather, but enough to flirt with your hairstyle — I placed the unfolded dollar into her hands, and asked, "What's your name?"

"Norma Jean," she said, with slight accent curling around her tongue.

"Norma Jean, that is so beautiful. I'm Aimee."

She reached out her hand to me. Cold. Piano fingers. Like breaded bones.

I wanted to ask her what she does when she's not leaning against the wall at the midpoint of the stairs headed toward the subway platform. I wanted to ask her what flavors remain in her mouth and if I should be bringing her breakfast instead of a dirty George Washington. I wanted to ask her what her favorite sound is or if she ever dressed up for Halloween or on days when she thinks there is no reason to wake, what wakes her. What brings her here? What concerns her?

But instead I just said, "Be well," knowing if I see her tomorrow, she made it another day. And frankly, I did too.

Last summer, I found a $20 bill on the sidewalk on my way somewhere I don't remember. I inhaled, exhaled, then scooped it up, deciding that without a name of ownership, it was fair game to throw inside my pocket and call it mine. I felt rich. *Really.* I thought of all the things I could buy with my newfound fortune. A cup of coffee, pastry and some carrot juice with enough for a generous tip. Lunch for me and my spouse (nothing too fancy, of course). Two or three shirts at my favorite thrift store. Almost a full tank of gas for a car. Seven trips on the subway.

I can't recall what I spent my $20 on, but it didn't last long. And when it was gone, it was as though it never existed.

Norma Jean has eyes like acorns. I stare into them and press my questions into her pupils. I think about remaining there with her, keeping her company as she collects dollar bills. We can make up stories about the people who pass us by. I can ask her what food she likes the best and how she prefers it prepared. Then, I can slip away and cook for her. Invite her over. Play her songs on ukulele while she sips her favorite blend of tea. Maybe she will want to take a nap or be alone or study a map to take her toward a land where it doesn't matter how many dollars you amass; everyone is treated equally. Food and housing for everyone!

As I approach her regular spot, I notice she is not there. Today, I have a dollar bill and an orange. Vitamin C that just needs to be peeled. I wonder where she is and if she is hungry or tired or happy or wandering. I wonder if she is leaning against a different wall of a different subway platform. Maybe she is still asleep.

With orange and dollar bill untouched, I walk toward the end of the platform, waiting for the train to come. I try not to worry about where Norma Jean might be. I glimpse into my bag and see evidence of my day ahead: student papers with my comments drizzled throughout, the poems we will be discussing today, dry erase markers, and my journal. I take it out and leaf through my random notes. I stop at the page where I wrote down Norma Jean's name. Before it, I wrote: *She told me her name today. Why did it take me so long to ask her?*

I skip to a blank page and write the date at the top. I peek my head toward the track to see if the train is coming. No lights. I have time. So I write:

*I read that Charles Baudelaire's last words were, "Cré nom!" which meant holy name! He had a massive stroke and spent his final years partially paralyzed. Could it be that in his final moments, he finally became aware of his sacred existence? What happens when we learn each other's names? They are no longer strangers to us. With exchange of just one word, we become connected.*

When the subway comes, I try not to worry about this person I do not even know. But maybe that is the problem. We forget about each other. And if there was some way we could all have each other's phone number or preferred location, we could make sure that someone somewhere was always checking in. Instead, we drop our eyes to palms and completely forget the lives and emotions breathing all around us.

I grab a seat and barely a few minutes pass before someone walks on the subway asking for change. Or food to eat. Or if you can't offer that, at least a smile. I finger Norma Jean's dollar in my pocket. I know that I can replace it.

The man shares a story about his wife (just died, leaving him unable to afford the rent alone) and his dog (ran away) and due to various injuries just cannot keep a job. So here he is, he tells us. Begging. Asking. Reminding us that we are just a few moments away from this.

I pull out Norma Jean's dollar and hand it to him. He smiles and I mirror one back. A few others give him what he asked for. Then, the day continues.

When I was 22, I sat on a bench in a small park in Manhattan, more well-known for its human-like sculptures than for its greenery. I was with my girlfriend at the time, and while she was reading her just-purchased comic book, I was writing in my journal. I looked up and noticed a man. Jesus tattoo on forearm. Wild eyes like sun-bleached blueberries. Swatting pigeons with his t-shirt, calling them *figeons*.

I started drawing him into my notebook using words. He noticed me notice him, and began moving closer to me.

"You writing about me?" he asked.

"Uh, yeah," I answered, cautiously. "And other stuff too."

My girlfriend-at-the-time barely noticed as Figeon (what else could I possibly call him) and I started learning about each other. He had a sometimes-place to stay in Queens. Mainly he slept on benches underground — on the subway platform. Or in the park, unless the cops were around. He told me that he was the king of this park and that he fought every day to keep this position. He showed me the giant scar on his back and the one on his shoulder and told me all about his son who played baseball but barely spoke to him. He told me that he didn't know how to read but if I were to read him a poem, he'd listen. He asked me if I was thirsty. Offered to buy me something to drink even though he had no money to purchase one.

I would visit Figeon anytime I was in the city. He was almost always there, even though I went on different days at different times. And when he wasn't there, everyone knew who I was because he called me the poet. On days Figeon wasn't there, I made other friends. Justin had tattoos on his fingers, crooked soft teeth and long hair he'd occasionally swat off his shoulders. There was also Matty and Robert and

Dina and others who gave me their stories. They all lived in this park.

When I get to school, I am still thinking about Norma Jean. I am also thinking about Figeon. When I walk into the classroom, I address the students. It is day two of our summer semester together. On the first day of class, as I called out their names, I asked them to permit me at least four or five classes before I knew all their names. "You only need to know one," I reminded them. "I've got almost 25."

And on this second day we are together, I am quite surprised that as I take roll call, I know just where to look.

"You remember!" one student said. "See, you thought it would take longer."

"You're right," I say. "Maybe it has something to do with your faces. How bright they are. And my desire to want to know you and not just point."

I didn't learn Figeon's given name until after almost a year of visiting him. I told him that I titled him Figeon in my notebook and he liked this, especially after I told him why.

His friends at the park had many names for him, but his mother called him Jimmy. I find it interesting that we have these different personas depending upon whom we are with and the names which accompany them.

To my students, I am Teacher. Or Professor. Sometimes Aimee, which I prefer.

Growing up, I always desired a nickname because I thought it equated closeness with the person calling us this. I yearned for more syllables in my name to make this easier. My sister occasionally calls me Aim and it fills me with joy.

I never got to say goodbye to Figeon.

I moved away from New York and was away for a few years. One January, I found myself back at that park. Snow covered the ground. Figeon was not there, but I recognized one of the regulars.

"Have you seen Fig— uh, Jimmy around much?" I asked.

"He died last August." He must have noticed the pain in my face, because he added, "I'm sorry, kid. Really."

Since I was a teenager, I've had a difficult time retaining friendships. I flee when it gets too serious. I'm not sure what to call these relationships we have with almost-strangers. The fleeting moments that are very often deeper than decade-long friendships. We are capable of revealing so much in just a handshake or shared conversation. Sometimes I think Figeon knew more about me than many of my friends at that time, and I barely told him much.

Even though I now know her name, I still know nothing about Norma Jean. Though, to be fair, she knows nothing about me too. But now we can exchange more than just a smile. And when I give her a dollar, she says, "Thank you, Aimee" and I say, "Be well, Norma Jean." It's like there is this delicate, almost-translucent thread that unites us now because we are more than just two humans in the same city, trying to find a way to exist. We can address each other like friends or like two people trying to find a way to remind the other that they are seen.

A.H.

## Rats v. Pigeons

"You think rats are beautiful?" he asked.

"No, actually I don't. But who gets to decide who or what lives or dies just based on beauty? Why should that even be a factor?"

*****

Fifteen minutes earlier I was alone on a bench in a park I had never been to before. The sun was muscular, but I had found a place in the shade to eat my leftover pasta from last night's dinner before it was time to go to therapy. It's almost impossible to be truly alone in New York City. There is noise and flapping limbs all around, but I felt like I had a window of quiet until—

An older man carrying two full grocery bags sat beside me. I immediately grumbled, angry by his intrusion. He was drinking from a tall can of beer — no paper bag covering, completely exposed. I tried to ignore him and breathe my practiced yoga breaths. In and out and in and out and (you get the idea).

In front of us, a woman scooped out heaping amounts of birdseed and rained it over the elevated flowerbeds. Suddenly, a swarm of pigeons swooped over and landed on the treats. It was actually quite magnificent to see: so many feathers and colors, and even the sound of all of them descending.

"You know, you're just encouraging the rats to come!" he yelled out to her. "This park is for *us*, not *them*!"

She turned around. A woman of about 70 in a wide-rimmed, white hat shading her face.

"There are no rats here," she said plainly.

"They come for what's left. All those seeds. Then when it gets dark, the rats come out. It's disgusting. You shouldn't do that."

I just wanted to eat my pasta and be introspective with the sun, but how could I ignore this?

"Actually, pigeons are like Labradors," I said, turning toward him. "They won't leave any food behind."

"Oh, I doubt that. She is doing a disservice to this city. I used to come to this park all the time, but the rats are just taking over."

The woman seemed unfazed by his annoyance.

I took a deep breath, already feeling the pasta curdling in my body.

"Look, clearly, it brings this woman great pleasure to feed the pigeons. Why do you care so much?"

"Don't you understand they are ruining our city!"

"The pigeons?"

He nodded.

"But they are so beautiful."

"You think rats are beautiful?" he asked.

"No, actually I don't. But who gets to decide who or what lives or dies just based on beauty? Why should that even be a factor? And you must realize that *we* are a factor as well."

"What do you mean?"

"We leave our garbage everywhere. Look under this bench. Crumbs and wrappers from whatever we ate, trash that we just toss on the ground because we are too self-centered or lazy to walk a few steps away toward a garbage can. You can't just blame the pigeons."

"They carry disease," he retorted.

"So do we. Should we start starving humans now?"

Of course, he had no reply for this.

Finished with my lunch, I grabbed my bag and said goodbye to this pigeon-hating man and walked toward the garbage can to throw away my napkin. The woman was leaning over the flowerbeds, and one of the pigeons had perched on her forearm. It looked like it was showing her gratitude.

"I, uh, I just wanted to thank you for what you're doing," I said to her.

The woman turned around and smiled at me. "Thank you."

"And I think you're wonderful," I added.

"Listen, I deal with guys like that all the time. In fact, I married one. There are no rats here."

"I believe you," I smiled back. "You know, pigeons are my spirit animal."

"What do you mean?"

I began to tell her the story of three years ago. Being around a blooming bonfire in a small town in Nebraska. The stars lit up overhead like faraway chandeliers and a group of new and not-yet friends sat around sharing the story of our spirit animals.

"I had never really thought about this," I said to the woman. "But it was a giant circle, so I had time to think before it got to be my turn. There were a few elephants and a cheetah, a falcon, a leopard and even a salamander. Then it got to me."

She put down her scoop and turned her entire body to face me, as though she really wanted to know my answer.

"I thought about people's descriptions of their chosen animal and why they chose what they chose. You know, like elephants are dedicated. Always searching for water. Resilient, even when hunted. A cheetah is fast, sleek."

"So why'd you decide on a pigeon?" Clearly, I had her attention.

"Well, when it got to me, all I could think about were pigeons. Living in the city, they are everywhere." I pointed to the mass crowd of them behind her and gestured. "And they, too, are resilient. I've seen pigeons missing a claw, a leg, with charred feathers, with swollen bellies. They don't give up. Beside all the other birds, they are seen as nuisances and diseased. 'Rats of the sky,' some call them."

"Shame on those people," she said. "They don't get it."

"Yeah, well, we think we understand each other ... we think we understand the creatures around us, but we really don't. Anyway, I actually said the carrier pigeon—"

"Homing pigeon," she interrupted.

"Yes, right! Because they were our first postal workers in the sky. They actually delivered mail — how miraculous, right? And their colors are unexpected and illuminating. They are so misunderstood."

The woman smiled. She grabbed my hand and squeezed it. "It's so rare to notice these things," she said. "It's why I feed them. Because there were times in my life that *I* went unnoticed. Times in my life when I could have used a good meal. We've got to remember to give it back."

She let go of my hand and turned back around toward the pigeons. She gave me enough of her time; the pigeons needed her now.

I smiled and slowly exited the park. I suddenly felt an odd gratitude toward the man on the bench because he brought these words out. And I wouldn't have connected with this woman had he not have interjected his pigeon hate speech.

Walking around New York City, it's impossible not to think about the imbalance of treatment toward each other. Some walk around with pockets full of disorganized money, while others have no pockets to fill. We walk past each other without regard. Pigeons are this beautiful reminder that in order to survive, we must hunt. Hunt for space. Hunt for food. Hunt for the (right) humans who understand us.

I still think rats are gross, and if one crossed my path (which has happened numerous times), I might emit a tiny scream. But outside, where they live, I would do my best not to get in their way. Because we all live here — regardless of beauty and wealth and likeability. That's what makes this city, this planet, this world so remarkable.

A.H.

# My Father

When I lost track of my mind, my father took me on a tour of Brooklyn. My hair stood like a giant knot on the top of my head. I looked like a weeping willow tree without the sturdy trunk. My appetite had hit the road, hiked outside of my body and I was beginning to recognize bones growing more prominent beneath my skin. There was no energy left inside me to live.

He insisted upon camping out at my apartment, sleeping on my not-quite-resembling-a-couch-futon. He refused to let me go, no matter how much pain I was in.

When I was younger, we'd rebel against my mother by going to garage sales. After scooping up the best loot we could find, my father would decide upon a lot fee. He was always the best bargainer. We'd fill up his car with random bits of someone else's trash that were now our coveted treasures with the silent realization that we'd have to hide whatever we got from my mom. She preferred new to old, and never quite understood the art of tag sales. Though I loved searching through other people's things, what I loved most was the time I got to spend with him. We developed a special language that sometimes just existed with the silent looks we exchanged.

When I was 35, I lost track of my mind and my father drove from Connecticut to Crown Heights to save me from drowning.

He decided to take me to Coney Island. It was April — warm enough to walk on the sand without socks, but early enough in the year that we felt like we owned the beach. Usually, I would have run toward the ocean, flirting with all the wildlife creeping its way out of the water. I'd collect shells and beach glass (careful not to confuse with sharp remnants of beer bottles). I would let my toes dig into the sand and get massaged by its texture. I would feel aware of all this, of all the life around me. Unfortunately, I felt gutted. Heartbroken. Relapsed within my depression.

Before we reached the beach, my dad drove us to Bensonhurst, Brooklyn, to where he used to live as a child. He parked the car by his old apartment and I suggested we knock on the front door to see if we could go inside.

The woman who answered the door spoke no English. She looked confused, staring at an old man and a frizzy redhaired depressive. We thanked her and kept walking.

When I was in my early 20s, I lived with my father for two years while I went to community college. It was the first time in my life that I did well in school. I was drug-free (mostly) and trying to remain focused and healthy.

My favorite memories of living with him consisted of trying out new recipes together, having late night chats when he would not-so-subtly wait up for me after a date. He saw me weather break-ups and then plummet into fierce love affairs. Our secret language extended its vocabulary and I felt like there was nothing I couldn't tell him that he wouldn't understand or accept.

That day in Bensonhurst, we slowly walked around. I don't remember where we stopped, or if we did. Maybe we only walked a few blocks. All I remember is how relieved I was that he let me roam. I couldn't make decisions; I could barely swallow food. But he gave me the best medicine of all: patience and time.

When I was 19 years old, I came out of the closet. Oddly enough, as a kid, I actually would hide in my closet. But I am speaking metaphorically. When I told my parents I was gay, I expected their eyes to jump out of their sockets from disbelief. We were at a Chinese food restaurant on my birthday and all they said was, "We knew. We've just been waiting for you to feel ready to tell us."

My father accepted every girlfriend I had. He asked no questions other than "Does she treat you with respect?" When I momentarily experimented with my sexuality and dated a man, my dad welcomed him too.

I have met so many people over the years who, because of their sexual orientation or gender identity, have been cast aside by their parents and family. Asked to leave. No longer welcome. Just for announcing who they are. Just for trying to live a life of certainty and authenticity.

When we arrived in Coney Island, we walked toward the beach. I took my shoes and socks off and tried to cure my numbness by reconnecting with the sandy earth. On any other day, we'd have gotten hot dogs and fries at Nathan's because it is practically a sin to go to Coney Island and not devour its coveted cuisine. But my appetite had curled up inside me and I could barely swallow the salty air.

There was another beachgoer who walked by us and my dad stopped him.

"Would you take our picture?" he asked.

I felt my body become a fist; I didn't want any photographic evidence of how I was feeling. Yet, I couldn't say this to my dad, knowing how important it was to him.

As I write this, I am staring at the photo, which I keep on my wall. He is behind me in a dark blue shirt with the blue, blue sky and matching ocean behind us. I don't remember smiling during that time in my life and yet, there I am in that photo with all my teeth exposed.

I am 19 years old; I am 24; I am 27. Each time I relapsed from drugs, my father was there. He never yelled at me because addiction is a disease and when was the last time you yelled at someone with cancer? He held my hand. He fed me. He gave me time and space to talk about why it happened.

My father never brings this up. He doesn't let my past overshadow my present. He accepts me for who I am in this moment and is open to the fact that I may change my mind tomorrow. He doesn't do this because he is my father; he does this because he is my friend.

I lost track of my mind and still have days where it goes missing. I have days where it is difficult just to walk outside. I have days where I cannot be around others, where I am afraid to be around myself. And when I feel this way, I call him. Or I write because that is another medicine I have prescribed to myself. My dad teaches me every day that lives can shift in a moment. Sometimes we can have what we need and then, it can vanish. Or walk away. The hardest part of life is remaining. Every day, my father teaches me the importance of sticking around, amidst the heartache, hunger pains, and sadness.

Years later, we went back to Coney Island. And we made up for that time I couldn't eat anything. Perhaps hot dogs are my medicine too.

A.H.

Aimee Herman and Martin Herman

# A Correspondence Between Two Writers

**Aimee:** What does love mean to you?

**Martin:** At this point in my life, it is peace of mind, being comfortable with another person. Total trust and satisfaction that can only come from knowing that you're with someone on the same wave length; this would not have been my answer 40 years ago, so I have come to believe that the definition of love really depends on your stage of life and is subject to change.

**A:** To me, love is messy. It is constantly learned and relearned. With each person I've loved, I've loved differently. And better.

---

**A:** Since writing three novels, you've been going out and selling your books — one at a time — establishing personal connections with each one of your readers. Tell me about what you've noticed as an avid people watcher. You give so much away to your readers with each page. What do they give to you?

**M:** I've become terribly aware of how rushed everyone seems to be, constantly rushing from point to point, without the appearance of knowing where they are hurrying to or from. Perhaps I see this more clearly because I am aware that I am slowing down. Now that I am older and writing books, I am forced to slow down ... to think through the mindset of my characters. Those who take the time to stop and talk — to listen, to share ... refresh me, especially the younger readers. The current generation asks very thought-provoking questions. Generally, they seem to think things through. Some of the older readers tend to think about times and places of their youth. I think they may be sharing so much of their inner thoughts with me because they know that they will probably never see me again. I don't judge, I listen.

**A:** What are some things that have surprised you that they've shared?

**M:** Many have shared a secret desire to write their own books. Others tie memories of specific books they have read to very special times in their lives. Yes, electronic readers are popular — very popular, but, more and more people are telling me how much they love the feel of the paper and the smell of the ink. That is coming from as young as 10 and 11 all the way up to full senior status.

---

**M:** Tell me what you had hoped would come out of this project [of writing this book together].

**A:** It was an opportunity to archive our words together. We lead such unnecessarily busy lives. Twenty-four hours in a day! That's a lot and yet we feel like we have no time to call each other or share a cup of coffee. Rather, we *think* we have no time. This book was a chance to encourage each other's creativity; to remind ourselves all the love swirling around us — literally and within our imaginations. Also selfishly, I wanted a book on my shelf that had both of our names on it.

---

**M:** Define a writer to me.

**A:** You want me to *name* a writer?

**M:** No. What does the word "writer" mean to you?

**A:** Well, I always go back to my students. I tell them: A writer writes. So often, we think of a writer as someone with a book.

Someone published. Someone famous. That's not what makes a writer. A writer is someone who thinks. Who takes the time to explore their thoughts and eventually gets it out on paper. A writer is someone who understands that the words may not arrive every day. Sometimes I go days without getting anything down on paper. But I am always thinking. And thinking is part of the writing process.

---

**M:** My mother, your grandmother, didn't get past eighth grade, and yet, there were always books in her hands, all kinds of books. When I do my appearances and signings and I hear people say "I don't read," they almost always follow the remark with a broad grin — like not reading is some badge of honor. I used to respond by saying "my condolences." Pretty snotty remark now that I think about it. I learned from my daughter — you — to say "well, maybe you just haven't found the right book yet." I like your comeback better than the one I gave initially. However, what I really have going through my head, is my mother saying, "when did you die or why are you starving your imagination?" You are an avid reader and truly love books, I wonder, what you *really* think when you hear people say that they don't read.

**A:** At the start of every semester, on the first day of class, I ask my students: Raise your hand if you're a writer. A few (if at all) tentatively raise their hand as though it's shameful. I ask the same question regarding if they are readers. Same response. I tell them: You are all writers. You are all readers. There are words all around you at all times. You just have to notice them. So, I give them time to widen their eyes and train or retrain themselves to notice. We often snicker or laugh when we are uncomfortable. Of course, we laugh when something is funny, too. But that discomfort is real and should be addressed. But never shamed. I've read books that after finishing them made me feel more alive. Made me want to write. Want to walk outside. Want to travel. Want to fall in love. Everyone is capable of feeling this too.

**M:** I'm not sure you answered my question. Tell me what it tells you to have a fair amount of people have the ability to say out in the open for anyone to hear — often with their own children next to them — I don't read. Then for them to smile or giggle about it.

**A:** [It tells me that] they haven't met their match. That they haven't given themselves a chance to fall in love with a book. A character. A poem. A story.

**M:** Let me ask it still a better way. I have no scientific proof one way or another but I would guess that a larger percentage of the population now reads less. We have fewer newspapers, fewer serious magazines, and we have an abundance of strongly one-sided opinions filling cable [television] and social media outlets. Too many of our population simply aren't well-informed anymore. And the problem with not being informed is the rulers begin to fill in the learning void with information that either seeks to frighten or misinform the population while they act in their own best interest. So what do *you* think? Is it true that a large percentage of the population isn't informed because they don't read, and if that is true, then what does that say about future generations?

**A:** I think it says that we have a lot of work to do. We need to pay our teachers more. We need to have better funding for our local libraries. We need more support and grants for independent presses so more is available to read. We cannot force people to read and frankly, that just pulls them away. We need to encourage. We need more spaces and people like you and me to remind those who are reluctant to pick up a book and read!

---

**M:** So we have tried to define love and we have tried to define literacy. How does the book we have just completed address either of those, if at all?

**A:** My hope is that readers who pick up this book see a bit of themselves in at least one of these stories. Someone who wakes up and feels like a stranger in their body reads "Dragonflies" and notes that gender doesn't have to be prescribed. Or someone reads "Finding Love at a Perfume Counter" and they chuckle at the ways in which the same story can be remembered in such different ways. Love is a giant noun with more definitions and shapes than one book could possibly contain. I just hope that by the end, the reader feels compelled to pick up another book or even write their own. We read to learn. We read to be entertained. We read to travel to worlds and cities we may not ever get to.

---

**A:** We've been talking about writing this book for quite a while. How do *you* feel about the final product?

**M:** For me there are two responses. One is the final product and the other is the process that created it. I expected to feel good about the process. I was hoping you would have the time to give that we could share together and that in itself would be a selfish gift to me. I was hoping that I would be able to firsthand witness what makes you the kind of a writer that I have always believed you to be. I have received all of that and so much more. I am so sorry that the project is almost over because I know that we will go our separate ways and for me, that is my loss. I am so very proud of you as a writer and I am so proud of you as a human being. I love the degree of honesty you express as you go from day to day and wish to come closer to it in my life. As far as the finished product is concerned, I think it has come out far better than I could have hoped it would be. It covers so many facets of love and the human experience. It covers sexuality and what we seek in our partners and what we are willing to give to them to make it more than a 50/50 relationship. The pieces and viewpoints you have brought to this book have helped me to increase my understanding of others. You mentioned that one of your objectives was to have a book on your shelf that bears both of our names. The fact that we created our own audio tape made it even better for me. Now I can hear not only your words but how you expressed them, I will probably play our tape over and over again. I hope people will read this book and understand the good nature that went into all of the pieces. I also hope it will make them think about what love means *to them*. Not just hormone-fed love, but conscience-fed love.

M.H./A.H.

# Also by Martin Herman: The Will James Mystery Series

### *The Jefferson Files*
the expanded edition
ISBN 978-1-945211-00-3 PRINT

It is 1806, early in Thomas Jefferson's 2nd administration. A deeply entrenched secret society arranges for a dissident within their organization to be brutally murdered and left floating in the Potomac River, within clear sight of the Jefferson White House.

Almost 200 years later, after discovering a lost diary written by someone who lived in the White House at the time of the crime, three college students and a world class computer hacker begin unraveling the modern-day offenses of the secret society. The students attract the attention of the modern-day leader of the secret society who threatens their very existence. Rather than retreat, the students fight back.

### *The Hidden Treasure Files*
ISBN 978-1-945211-01-0 PRINT

In *The Hidden Treasure Files*, Will James and his crew are asked to help unravel a mystery that begins in a Brooklyn antique store's weekly auction and ends in the most unlikely of locations. It should have triggered many questions when one specific auction attracts a room full of first time bidders. The auctioneer offers up a prohibition era permit, and to his surprise, two separate people quickly bid the price up to $100,000. The item is worth much more than that – to a very select group of people – including the current head of one of New York's crime families.

## *The Sweet Revenge Files*
ISBN 978-1-945211-02-7 PRINT

A bomb goes off in a crowded movie theater on Christmas Eve. Investigators quickly find fingerprints and DNA belonging to a convicted murderer. But 80 years before, this convicted murderer was executed. So, how could his fingerprints and DNA get all over this crime scene, *and* the getaway car? One thing is certain, you will be sitting on the edge of your seat until the very, very, last page.

# Also by Aimee Herman:

## *meant to wake up feeling*
(great weather for MEDIA, 2014)

Aimee Herman's powerful new collection addresses the complexities of identity, gender, memory, and body image. This is a book of surprise, humor, intimacy, fallibility, renewal. A treasure map of metamorphosis. Anne Waldman writes, "Visceral, insistent, beyond transgressive … Gratitude to Aimee Herman for getting under our skin, and moving poetry-in-discourse into the feminist present and future where we study and yearn for the salvation of humanity." Herman's work takes you on a personal journey of understanding a body's identity and, in turn, helps us understand who we are. These poems revel in Cummings' forms, Bukowski directness, and Kerouacian playfulness. For a generation set on defining itself, this book is a step in the right direction of realizing the only definition is ourselves. In Herman's own words, "Walk away from formula, resuscitate the dark inside, look for new bulb of light."

### *rooted, chapbook*
(dancing girl press, 2014)

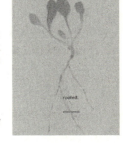

Poems meditating on various ways to look at/communicate with the body.

### *to go without blinking*
(BlazeVOX books, 2012)

Aimee Herman is a cyborg. Not in the sense of a mixture but: in her impetus. Her desire for a book to be a new kind of thinking and being in the world." As she writes in the startling Statement of Poetics that opens this passionate collection: "This body of text practices trilingualism and contraction. Gender is best received in a question mark." This is re-wiring where it counts: below the lexicon. Below the public-private register: "where the label was rubbed." Until there's nothing left but, as the writer says: "The most dangerous parts of me." A book in which *words* and beloveds, of various kinds: "never stop coming." What kind of cyborg is this?"

**To order printed copies
or e-books of any Martin
Herman novel, please
go to Amazon or visit
martinhermanauthor.com**

**Aimee Herman's works are
available through Amazon
& selected bookstores,
or by contacting Aimee at
aimeeherman@gmail.com**

**Your comments and suggestions are always welcomed.**

**Please visit Martin Herman's Web site: martinhermanauthor.com**

**Go to Martin's blog: mhermanwriter.wordpress.com**

**Like his Facebook page: Martin Herman-Writer**

**Or send Martin an e-mail via mherman194@prodigy.net**

**Please contact Aimee Herman at aimeeherman@gmail.com**

**Or visit the Web site: aimeeherman.wordpress.com**